Sailor

Sailor

Destiny Diaries

Delores Leggett Walker

Dream Publication

Dream Publication
Sailor
Copyright © 2016 by Delores Leggett Walker
This title is also available as a Kindle eBook
Cover photograph: Monica L. Walker
Cover design: Jason Taylor
Editors: Leta Turner and Jonnie Whittington
Author's photo: Megan W. Zipperer

Printed in the United States
Library of Congress Cataloging in Publication Data
Walker, Delores Leggett
Sailor/ Delores Leggett Walker
p.cm. – (Destiny Novellas); bk.1)
ISBN: 153683209X
Man-Woman/relationships/Fiction/Christian
fiction/Love stories.

For my daughter, Vickie, who felt the link of destiny with Sailor from the moment they met.

This one is for you with love.

Mama

Words are the Spoken Photos of the Soul

DLW

Her virtue was stolen on a cool autumn afternoon, as the wind rustled the live oak trees and the air smelled rich with the Louisiana bayou mud after a recent rain. The swaying moss in the trees mourned her loss with its ghost-like grey color that dripped with moisture as if the trees had seen her tragedy and wept with her.

Sailor Corbin, lay silent on the soggy ground, her eyes devoid of the tears locked deep in her soul.

At twelve years old she knew all the warnings about taking the short-cut through the woods coming home from school, but the lure of laughter caused her to throw caution to wind. She detoured off the well-traveled path for only a moment; drawn in by the familiar voices. The day quickly turned into the nightmare of the blackest night she'd ever known.

1

Sailor Corbin didn't like endings or beginnings. She liked to stay somewhere in the middle of things where there were no jolting starts or screeching halts. This safe area in the middle of life allowed her to live life on her own terms, doing what she wanted, whenever she wanted.

But, what if she had been wrong?

Meeting Pastor Alex Collins had shaken her, causing her to think that beginnings could be a magical place to live. As for the ending, time was the master of that. Right now, she needed to choose whether she wanted to see how this relationship would play out or simply walk away and once again settle for the way of life she'd led since she was twelve years old.

The phone shrilled, piercing her thoughts.

"Dr. Daughtry Corbin's office, Sailor speaking, May I help you?"

She recognized the low chuckle on the phone and smiled when Alex said, "I need to speak with the most beautiful person in the room please."

Sailor's cheeks warmed. She rolled her eyes but played along by coyly saying, "There is no one but me in the room."

Alex cleared his throat, suddenly shy at his forward comment that had brought such a tempting response from Sailor. He tugged at his shirt collar. It threatened to choke him as he envisioned Sailor sitting at her desk in a dress that probably hugged her curves, with her tangle of curls cascading around her shoulders like a midnight waterfall.

He had already resigned himself to the fact that he was falling deeply in love with Sailor. The problem was, he didn't know if she was willing to accept his gift of love. So far, every time he had tried to express his feelings towards her she had retreated into a place within herself, shutting him completely out. As a pastor, Alex had seen the scared look of apprehension on the faces of countless individuals he'd counseled over the years. He knew from experience, whatever Sailor was hiding would have to be settled before they had a chance to pursue a possible life together.

"Earth to Alex . . . you there?"

Doubts flooded his heart as he covered up his thoughts with laughter. "Here and accounted for. Now, let me get to the reason for my call. The town of Peron is holding their annual Blossom Festival next month. I thought perhaps you and Daughtry might enjoy coming." Alex rushed on before she could say anything. "I mean, that is, if you want to come. It is a wondrous time of the year in the North Georgia Mountains with everything starting to bloom. Frank and Mary will be here to visit their Cook relatives, and I'd love to have you visit my church . . ." he trailed off as he heard her soft intake of breath.

"Sailor, are you alright?"

He heard her take a ragged breath before she gently said, "Alex, are you sure you're ready to introduce me to your congregation?"

"Why on earth would you say that, Sailor?"

"Well, I'm Creole and you pastor a church in a small Georgia town. Some folks could have memories from the past that shape their opinion of their pastor dating a woman of color."

Alex heard the hurt in her voice. It was at that moment that he realized their journey to a life together would not be an easy road to travel, but nevertheless, with God's help, and if Sailor would agree, they could walk it together, one step at the time.

"This is not the way I planned to tell you this, but, Sailor, I am falling in love with you and I would be honored if you would consider coming to my hometown so I can introduce you to my world. My hope is that it will become your world as well."

Sailor wiped the tears from her cheeks, humbled by the compassion in Alex's declaration of love. She had no idea why she'd brought up the race-card. Her best friend, Vickie was white, plus Alex had shown that he didn't have a prejudice bone in his body. She knew her racially charged question was a smoke-screen to cover her real feelings for him. She was terrified to even recognize such feelings. Nor was she ready to explain to this good man she was damaged goods, that she had a family curse on her, and that she had sworn to never fall in love with anyone for fear of contaminating them with her horrible secrets.

2

With a sigh, Sailor turned away from her desk. She planted her feet firmly on the floor and stood. She took deep breaths to cleanse her mind from the hideous memories the conversation with Alex had dredged up.

Heaviness lay in her stomach as she walked over to look out the window.

The courtyard in front of the office complex was just like it was every day. Folks were out and about, tending to business in the more than a dozen buildings surrounding her brother's Antiquities office. Daughtry had taken a week off to fly to South Dakota. He planned to meet up with a team of archeologist at a site where a pre-historic village was recently discovered. The lure of being on the ground floor of a new discovery was more than he could turn down.

She let out the breath she'd been holding. What was wrong with her? Why in the world was she all bothered and upset? The past months had been great. She'd come to know Alex as a person of tremendous integrity and strength. Added to that winning combination was his sense of humor, his easy-going personality. Best of all, he never pushed Sailor to give more than she was capable of giving.

That is . . . until today.

The door opened. She recognized the dark hair sprinkled with premature grey that glistened like silver when her friend, Vickie, poked her head inside the opening and said, "Get out here quick. This has got to be the cutest thing I've ever seen."

She disappeared from the doorway. Sailor had no choice but to follow if she was to find out the source of her friends excited comment. She focused on Vickie's bright orange shirt and followed her to where a small crowd was gathered near the stone fountain in the center of the courtyard.

"No way," Sailor exclaimed as she saw a small brown monkey sitting on the edge of the fountain. It was eating a banana as if it didn't have a care in the world.

Vickie laughed. "Yes way, now the question is who wants to tell him to move along, that he can't take up residency in a public place." She clapped her hands in glee and watched the tiny monkey tilt his head sideways and copy her hand motion, clapping every time Vickie clapped.

Sailor's spirits lifted. The unexpected moment of hilarity was just what she needed to forget Alex's call, and to let go of the disturbing thoughts that tried to spoil her day.

The crowd shifted when someone called out, "Bobo, you little monkey, get over here this minute."

Cell phones flashed as photos were snapped of the prissy little monkey politely jumping off the edge of the fountain to saunter towards the man who'd called its name. The monkey jumped from the ground to the man's arm. He crawled

16

effortlessly to his shoulder and locked an arm around the man's neck. A toothy grin from Bobo was the last thing they saw as the two walked away.

"Just a monkey and his friend out for a stroll," Vickie giggled.

Sailor looked at her wrist watch. "Let's go to lunch. I know it's only eleven o'clock, but I'm hungry and if we go early we can beat the crowd."

"You took the words right out of my mouth. I'll get my purse and meet you at your office in five minutes."

They walked the two blocks to the small café that was a favorite of the downtown crowd. You had a choice of eating inside or at one of the four tables outside. Sailor and Vickie always preferred outside, especially on a spring day like this when the air was as soft and warm as a baby's skin.

Two of the tables were taken by college kids that were communicating separately on their phones. They appeared to be totally unconcerned they occupied the same space.

Vickie leaned over to stage-whisper in Sailor's ear. "It's the modern version of eating with friends and family where the cell-phone is the main attraction."

Sailor nodded her agreement. "Snag us the table in the corner and I'll order for us. You want the usual?"

Vickie pouted her lips. "Yeah, just salad as I bravely fight the good fight with my fat cells."

Sending her a poor-baby look, Sailor promised to fill their plates from the salad bar and sneak a double helping of fruit salad on the side.

Holding their plates, she walked to their table slowly, and watched sunbeams, filtered by the lattice wall scatter bursts of light around the café patio.

It was a beautiful Florida morning.

Vickie blessed the meal and Sailor smiled at the obvious pleasure her friend derived from the abundant plate. Noticing her perusal, Vickie continued to chew. She swallowed, and then said, "What?"

Sailor offered her upturned hand. With the understanding of a true friend, Vickie placed her hand in hers and said, "I know, I love you too. You are the best dieting buddy ever. Here you are eating salad when you could eat a million calories a day without gaining a pound."

"Okay, believe that if you must, but you know my weakness and how I can't pass the Ole Candy Shoppe without stopping. I am convinced the smell of chocolate creates a chemical reaction like a time-released drug in my body. I've come to believe moderate amounts of chocolate will keep me from aging and my body will thank me one day," Sailor reasoned.

"Hmmm . . . you will not turn to fat," Vickie said to the food as she stared at the bite of fruit salad on her fork.

"You silly goose, have you looked in the mirror lately? Your dark hair with its snowflake sparkles, luminous hazel eyes, and a smile that lights up the world makes you drop-dead gorgeous. Now, enough with the fat worries, I want to hear about your latest conquest."

Vickie grinned with pleasure as she told Sailor about Mason Butler. Sailor knew he was a film-maker that Vickie had met when they'd literally collided with each other as she'd stepped into the elevator as he was stepping out.

"He's all spit and polish in his three-piece suit, but underneath the shine is a heart that enjoys the simple life just like mine," Vickie said.

"Aww, Vickie that is the sweetest thing. Maybe he's your soul-mate. Bring him by the office to meet me."

"I'll do that just as soon as he gets back in Tallahassee. He had to make a trip home to the Panhandle to some kind of fund-raiser for kids."

Sailor asked why he was in Tallahassee. Vickie told her he was there to scout out locations for his Christian film company.

"Oh my word, he makes movies – maybe he wants to make you a star!"

"Well, lawdy da, maybe he does," Vickie teased as she flipped her shiny hair with her hand in a mock movie-star gesture. She said, "Okay enough about my love life; I want to hear about you and Pastor Alex."

Sailor shrugged her shoulders. "I don't think Alex and I are meant to be."

Vickie leaned towards Sailor with concern etched on her face. "You can't possibly mean that. I've seen the way you look at each other. What brought this change of heart since we talked yesterday?"

Sailor froze. All she could hear was the beating of her heart and the sudden rush of blood pounding in her ears. How could she explain something she didn't understand herself?

3

Vickie glanced at Sailor as they walked back towards the office complex. She was a good enough friend to keep her thoughts to herself. She knew this somber attitude was unusual for Sailor who was normally upbeat and easy-going.

Before she left Sailor, Vickie squeezed her hand and said, "Call me if you want to talk about this."

She saw the closed look in Sailor's eyes and hugged her. "I'm your friend, right? That means you can trust me with whatever is causing you pain."

Sailor watched her walk away. The lump of sadness in her throat was physically painful as she grappled with the overwhelming desire to run after Vickie and try to explain the complex feelings that had surfaced when Alex called this morning. It reminded Sailor of a pot of water on a stove burner as it started to simmer around the edges and then burst into a boiling roll as the heat intensified. She knew Alex didn't have a mean bone in his body and that he would never intentionally cause pain to anyone, but, his declaration of love stirred up memories she desperately needed to keep buried for her peace of mind.

Sailor unlocked the door and went into the office. With Daughtry out of town and no urgent appointments on the books, she planned to spend the afternoon catching up on the filing she'd let slip. She didn't have the OCD gene like her brother, but she liked things to be in reasonable order. Determined to lay her demons to rest while doing something productive, Sailor grabbed the stack of files and placed them on her desk.

She paused to look at the photograph of the antique Double-Wedding Ring quilt in the file on top. Sinking into her chair, she scanned the notes Daughtry had written about the first visit Loren

Taylor had made to their office. Sailor remembered it as if it were yesterday. Loren had arrived with a large tote bag in her hand. When she'd pulled the quilt from the bag it felt like a calming presence had walked into the room. Sailor remembered how she was instantly drawn towards the colorful quilt and laid her fingers against the delicate pattern of the fabric. The first contact with the quilt had sent tingles in her fingers, even as a peaceful calmness had settled all over her. Sailor found out later that Loren's quilt held healing properties, and had the exact affect on all who touched it.

She stroked her fingers across the photograph willing it to bring the same level of peace she'd experienced that day. It didn't of course. It was just a likeness of the real object that was in Colton and Loren's daughter Maggie's room back in Monroe.

"Maybe I need to make a trip to Monroe," Sailor whispered.

Shaking her head in derision at the futility of wishful thinking, Sailor filed the paperwork. The dozen or so other files were put away quickly, not holding the same level of interest as the one that included her personally when she become a part of the Destiny Foundation. The foundation had opened doors for so many deserving people since it was birthed from the *Legend of Promise* left to her friend Loren.

Twenty minutes later, the door opened and a well-dressed matron walked inside. She introduced herself as Mrs. Ella Martin. The first thing Sailor noticed was her large brown eyes that reminded her of the soft velvet of a mink's fur.

"Nice to meet you, Mrs. Martin, be seated please," Sailor said.

Mrs. Martin smiled, creating tiny lines at the corners of her expressive eyes.

"Let's don't stand on formalities, dear. Call me Ella," she said.

"Thank you Ella."

Ella sat in the chair in front of Sailor's desk. Her regal bearing was re-enforced by the cultural tone of her soft southern drawl when she asked to speak with Dr. Daughtry Corbin. Sailor told her he would be out of town for several days.

"How may I help," Sailor asked.

"Thank you my dear. Perhaps you can help me. I live in Thomasville, Georgia, and as you can see my advancing age has slowed me down a bit. My precious husband has been gone from this world many years and we were never blessed with children to carry on the family fortune." She leaned forward as if to share a secret with Sailor. "Now, this is my dilemma. A childhood friend died recently in Port St. Joe, Florida. Much to my sorrow we didn't visit very often in recent years since neither of us could see well enough to drive long distances. When I was contacted of her death last week, I learned her wish was to be cremated and her ashes scattered in the Gulf of Mexico. I was also informed she had left all her worldly possessions in my care. The plain truth is, I don't know if I've inherited a treasure or a pile of junk and I need someone with your brother's knowledge to travel with me to see what is there."

Compassion for the elderly lady stirred in Sailor's heart. She reminded her of her Creole grandmother Elise Leclere, who died when Sailor was twelve. They had the same air of quiet authority in the dignified way they carried themselves, and the cultural tone of their voice. The phrase . . . *a steel hand in a velvet glove* popped into her mind as she compared the two women. It described both of them to a T.

Sailor felt a stab of nostalgia when she thought of Grandmere. Ella stopped talking and looked at her for a moment, until Sailor managed to bring her mind back to the present.

"I'm sorry for the loss of your friend. Please tell me if there is anything I can do to help until my brother returns."

"Well, as you know, we live in a world now-a-days where some folks have no respect for other's property. I had not even thought of this until just now, but it seems like a perfectly sensible suggestion to ask if you would be inclined to travel with me to my friend's house tomorrow and have a look at the items. I plan to list the property with a realtor in Port St. Joe but I feel compelled to honor my friend by going through her belongings before strangers purchase her house."

The words *Do it Shae Bebe'* . . . whispered inside her head in a voice that sounded surprisingly like her sweet Creole grandmother's voice.

On impulse, Sailor told Ella she would be glad to accompany her on her trip. Maybe it would be the perfect solution to erase the troubling snatches of memory that played around the edges of her mind. She had played this mind game for several years and knew that filling her hours with other projects was the best way to keep the alarming wolves of that fateful day at bay. Yes, she decided, a good day's distraction was exactly what she needed.

4

Sailor fought the yawn tickling her throat. She stretched her legs until her toes touched the spindles at the foot of her bed. Drawing her feet back from the smooth iron surface of the centuries old bed frame she pondered her quick decision yesterday to accompany someone on a trip that she had only met once. Not coming up with a single valid reason other than her gut dictated she go, she decided it didn't matter. A day out of the norm couldn't hurt once in a while.

She gazed at the brightness of the new day spreading squiggly patterns across the matching white dresser and chest of drawers. As the only granddaughter in the Corbin family, the furniture was given to her after Grandmere died.

The antique bed had been her place of comfort long before it was brought to her bedroom. Memories of snuggling in the softness of the feather mattress, twice the depth of modern mattresses reached back to times when Sailor couldn't have been more than one or two years old. On those special occasions Grandmere would whisper secrets about growing up in New Orleans. Wondrous tales about her grandmothers dating from the time the family had left their homeland in Canada to find a new home in the boggy wetlands of southern Louisiana.

The colorful stories of the women included her ancestor Rosette. Grandmere said Sailor could pass for Rosette's twin, and that she had been the most beautiful woman to attend the Quadroon Balls at the Orleans Ballroom.

Family history said she became the Placee of a wealthy white planter and lived as a kept woman on Ramport Street in New Orleans. Their union produced several children who become influential leaders in Louisiana.

The accepted culture of her ancestor always sounded romantic to Sailor. When Grandmere described the formal gowns Rosette wore that were made of whisper soft tulle and crisp satin, Sailor could almost feel the gown slipping over her head as she prepared to attend the Ball. She would sway to the inner sound of the music, becoming one with the story of her look-alike ancestor . . . that is until the fateful day she was raped.

After that day, she began to see the abuse leveled against her as part of a curse passed down from Rosette who was helpless to choose a life beyond the one chosen for her. Her parent's determination to keep the attack a secret added to her weight of guilt. Somehow their silence made her feel she was responsible for the rape, instead of the teenage boys who had held her captive; helpless in the face of the most horrendous terror she'd ever known.

Remembering set her on edge. She tossed the covers aside, and propped up on the pillows to make a half-hearted plea to God. Without really believing He could help her, she went ahead anyway and asked Him to take away the raw feelings she'd had ever since Alex's call yesterday.

To her surprise, Sailor felt calmness immediately. She believed in God, but wasn't one to seek Him at every turn. It just wasn't in her nature to depend on God. Sailor preferred to chart her own course in life, depending on reason instead of the ethereal world of prayer. Or at least that's what she told herself.

Truth was, she didn't feel worthy to bother God. Those old tangled feelings of being less than pure made her reluctant to communicate with God.

But, for some reason she decided to test the waters to see if God was really listening to her.

Scooting over to sit on the edge of the bed she said, "Uh, God, I don't want to bother you, but, if you're listening I'd like to know what you think about me driving Ella to Port St. Joe today?"

A verse from her Sunday School days flashed across her mind. *Do unto others as you'd have them do unto you . . .*

She shook her head in surprise, and then decided the answer was a fluke. She was sure God was too busy running the universe to talk to her.

After all, she was an independent, single woman, living life on her own terms. She could handle her decisions.

By the time she had dressed and was on the way to the office she'd put the morning's conversation with God on the back burner of importance. After opening the office she checked the messages on the answering machine. She didn't have to return any calls, so she dialed Ella's home phone and told her she'd pick her up within the hour.

Placing the *Closed for the Day* sign on the door, Sailor locked the door and went to the parking garage where she'd parked her car. She unlocked the car and slid behind the wheel for the drive to Thomasville.

She made the short drive to Thomasville and found Ella's residence on the outskirts of town less than ten minutes after arriving. Slowing her car she turned into the circular drive of a vintage Georgia mansion. It was magnificent.

"Oh wow," Sailor breathed. She opened her car door and walked slowly to the porch as she admired the house and surrounding rose gardens. Her soft rap on the door was answered while her fist was still in motion.

"Come right in," said the woman who'd opened the door.

Sailor saw she was somewhat plump, and dressed in a medium blue pin-striped shirtwaist that matched her eyes.

Her denim-blue eyes gazed steadily at Sailor. "I'm Elizabeth Beckett, Ella's housekeeper. I'll let her know you have arrived. She is beyond excited to finally be going to Port St. Joe," she said as she motioned for Sailor to have a seat in the living room.

Sailor sat on the edge of a pink damask sofa near the entryway. She hummed as she waited. It was an annoying habit that showed up when she was nervous, and one she'd failed to break even though she knew it was a childish reaction.

From her jacket pocket, her cell chirped. The caller ID flashed Daughtry's name and number.

"Daughtry, what's happening," she asked with concern knowing it was very early in South Dakota because of the time difference.

Sailor could hear the wonder in his voice when he spoke. "We found the site around midnight and so far the dig has turned up at least a dozen complete fossils. It looks like an entire village in the valley. Something happened. It's like the people were stopped dead in their tracks."

"Good Lord . . ." Sailor managed to squeak out.

"Right. I couldn't wait a second longer to share the news with you. The news media is sure to have caught wind of the activity and will be here soon in droves. I wanted you to hear it from me first."

"I am so happy for you brother. I guess this means you'll be staying out west a little longer than you planned."

"Yes, at least until we determine what we have here. That is, if there isn't any pressing issue I need to handle in Tallahassee right away."

Sailor glanced up to see Elizabeth and Ella standing in the doorway. She smiled at them and answered Daughtry. "We're good here. No pressing business. If something comes up I'll give you a call. Love you."

When she hung up, Ella said, "I pray all is well, my dear."

Sailor stood, her heart warmed at the kindness in her voice. "All is well, Ella. Are you ready to find out what is waiting for you in Port St. Joe?"

Ella pressed her fingers to her chest. "Yes, I am ready. But first, let me tell you that Elizabeth, who listens closely to God's voice, believes this trip is going to reveal much more than a houseful of belongings, and that it's imperative you accompany me. I can't help but agree since I've had the same inkling since our introduction yesterday. We were meant to meet, of that I am absolutely sure."

Her thoughts echoed the same words, but she didn't give voice to them. She preferred absolutes when dealing with everyday events. Sailor wasn't ready to admit that God might have arranged the meeting.

5

They made small talk as they traveled past Tallahassee and then turned west on Highway 98. Finding they had a lot in common even though they were generations apart, Sailor was content to drive and listen to Ella talk about growing up in Thomasville until she said, "Elizabeth believes you are struggling with unresolved issues."

Sailor's eyes went wide. "I beg your pardon. What did you say," she asked pretending she'd not heard the comment.

Ella smiled. "I believe you heard correctly my dear. Elizabeth is rarely wrong in her inner feelings. God reveals things to her as she prays. When your heart is ready to listen you'll hear His voice too."

Sailor tightened her gripe on the steering wheel. Everything in her wanted to ask Ella how she was so sure about her faith in God, but she couldn't. Her years of denial had erected a wall of defense against anything that threatened to reveal the hurt inside her.

Ella saw her reaction, and wisely turned the conversation in a different direction. They talked about the weather, likes and dislikes of certain foods, and current news for the next several miles.

Sailor slowed the speed of her car as they approached Carrabelle. The town was just one of the many small communities that dotted the Gulf coastline along Highway 98. Right after telling Ella a friend of hers and Daughtrys lived in the area and owned a local bread franchise she heard a horn toot at her from the side of the road. Sailor tapped the car brake and then pulled into the Dollar General parking lot when she saw their friend Edward waving at her. She pulled the car up beside him and let her car window down.

"Where you headed?" Edward asked.

Sailor introduced him to Ella and then told him they were on the way to Port St. Joe for the day.

"How are Leigh and the kids? Is Levi still catching more fish than you?"

Edward chuckled. "Leigh's fine, Shae is already acting like a teenager, Miss Ellie is a pistol with a capitol P, and as much as I hate to admit it Levi out fishes me most of the time."

Grinning at his humorous description of his children still living at home, Sailor asked about the three older daughters and their families.

He laughed. "The grandkids are growing too fast. We met up for a family get-together recently, ate boiled peanuts and had a blast swimming all afternoon!"

They chatted a while longer and said goodbye with a promise to visit soon. Sailor gave him a thumbs-up as she pulled back onto the highway.

When they crossed the bridge, Ella leaned forward to look at the large number of boats moored in the canal on the left side of the road.

"My dear husband and I always dreamed of owning a sailboat. We planned to retire and sail the oceans of the world, but fate got in the way through illness and he was taken way too soon."

Pain threaded through Sailor's voice as she imagined the how it would feel to lose Alex. "You must have felt so abandoned."

Something softened in Ella's expression. "Yes, there are still moments when I long for a different outcome, but those are the times I rest in my faith, and turn my thoughts to the many wonderful years we had together. I do so wish we'd been blessed with children, but it was not to be. Instead, God has given me Elizabeth and the precious folks of Thomasville."

"Tell me about your town. I come to the Rose Parade every year and have always wondered how it became such a well known event."

Ella smiled. "As a matter of fact, I attended the very first Rose Show."

"You did? Is it that old?" A blush flushed Sailor's cheeks. "Oh, I didn't mean to indicate you are old."

"Well, I am that old, and I am thankful for every year. Now, would you like to hear the story of the oldest Rose Show in the state of Georgia?"

Sailor heard the gentle rebuke, but wasn't offended. Like most young adults it was difficult for her to imagine living well into the decade before the century mark. She glanced at Ella and saw the twinkle in her wise brown eyes. They commanded respect, and still held a spark of mischief at knowing she'd made her point about age.

Ella held her gaze until Sailor said, "I'd love to hear the history behind the event. You know my brother and I specialize in preserving the things that shaped our world. Besides that, roses are my favorite flowers. I was hooked from the very first Rose Show I attended after moving to Tallahassee."

Their conversation lagged as they drove into Apalachicola. It was just as Sailor remembered it. The streets were clean and the downtown section was barely more than a half-dozen blocks of tidy storefronts displaying their wares to draw tourists into the stores to shop. She and Daughtry had visited the town when friends had told them about the historic Gibson Inn. Their stay at the Inn had turned into a lively get-together when several of the guests joined them on a walking tour of the town.

Their walks had taken them past the lovely houses, many were now Bed and Breakfast places, and as far as the centuries-old cemetery at the edge of town. They'd spent a full hour walking among the ancient tombstones. They'd placed parchment paper against the tombstone's engravings and had traced the poetic words from mourners of long ago. Sailor had placed her engravings in a photo album until she found time to write a travel book highlighting some of the most scenic places in North Florida.

A few minutes later as Sailor followed the winding curves hugging the coastline, Ella continued her story. She said she was a baby the first time she attended the Rose Show.

"Mama was a member of the Women's Garden Club in Thomasville. She said Thomas County's first Home Demonstration Agent, along with two other ladies created an exhibit for the State Fair at Macon in 1920. The exhibit won twenty-five dollars and the money was given to the Garden Club to start a flower show, preferably a rose show. Several Thomasville citizens met to plan the event and the first Rose Show was held in Neel's Department Store in April of 1922."

Ella chuckled, "Of course, I was much too small to remember the historic event, but Mama assured me I stole the show when she leaned close to a magnificent bouquet of red blooms and I began to nibble the petals with gusto."

"You ate the roses," Sailor exclaimed gleefully.

"Oh yes, and I love the taste and texture of rose petals to this day."

Sailor was so engrossed in Ella's account of the many Rose Show's she'd been involved in over the years, serving as the chairperson for a number of those years, that she was startled to realize they had arrived in Port St. Joe. The traffic light turned red as she eased to the intersection.

"You'll turn right here, Sailor. We are going to Douglas Landing just a few miles down the road."

The light changed to green, and Sailor turned right. Ella reminisced about the last time she'd visited her friend.

"The house is quiet large. It has three stories with more than twenty rooms."

Sailor tapped the brakes as a small squirrel skittered across the road in front of them. The area was North Florida at its best with miles of trees and thick foliage on both sides of the two-lane road. An occasional dwelling could be seen, nestled in the thicket with tree lined driveways leading to their front doors. It looked so peaceful to Sailor. Nothing like the postcard images of Florida showing miles of sandy beaches and sparkling waves rolling towards shore. This part of Florida, with its timber and wildlife, made you imagine you were in the backwoods of the mountains. Minus the mountains of course, but you still got the feeling of being cut off from civilization with its miles of natural habitat untouched by modern culture.

Not wanting to be nosey by asking too many questions, Sailor kept quiet, but she couldn't imagine anyone having a house with so many rooms.

Ella glanced at her and said, "Daisy loved to build and she kept adding rooms until she ended up with a house that has three stories and twenty-three rooms as I recall."

Leaning forward, Ella said, "Slow down a bit. I believe the lane is right about . . . yes, there it is. Right there to the left."

Sailor eased her car into the opening that was surprisingly well maintained with tall pine trees growing on each side of the lane. She followed the smooth surface and gasped in delight when the lane ended and she got her first glimpse of the extraordinary house.

The three stories of the buttercup-yellow house rose into the air surrounded by a cloudless blue sky. It looked like a photograph of a do-it-yourself home magazine cover. Whimsical flower boxes with red geraniums spilling over the edges graced the front windows on the ground floor that were framed with snowy white shutters to match the white shingle roof.

The second and third stories had over-sized windows that wrapped around the corners of the house with one spectacular shutter-framed window in the center of each level.

The entire structure was set in the center of a gardener's dream. Grass so green it looked like the covering of a high-dollar pool table was dotted with flowers blooming profusely. Bird baths were abundant and every tree appeared to have at least one bird feeder suspended from its limbs.

Ella saw the astonished look on Sailor's face. "It's just as I remember. Sweet Daisy always was an over-achiever."

6

As soon as Sailor walked into the house, she stopped to look around at what appeared to be a photograph of an 18th century drawing room. She sighed sweetly. "Oh my, your friend Daisy was an avid collector."

Ella smiled, her face softened as she remembered her visits with Daisy. She moved slowly into the room, dark with shadows. Going to the front window she opened the drapes allowing the sunlight to enter. Sailor could tell Ella missed her friend by the way she caressed the back of a velvet wing-back chair in deepest eggplant purple, and then walked over to open a music box. The box sat amongst a collection of what surely were antique figurines grouped together on a mahogany drop-leaf table.

The lilting sounds of classical music from the open box brought tears to Ella's eyes. At a loss for words, Sailor closed her eyes and imagined Daisy in the same room sharing the moment with them.

Ella talking brought Sailor back to the present when she asked, "How will I ever decide what is valuable to a collector and what is merely keepsakes?"

"Well, if the entire house is anything like this room I'd say you have inherited a gold mine."

Ella tilted her head and tapped her perfectly manicured fingernail against her chin. She looked seriously at Sailor with warm brown eyes. "But, I don't need a gold mine, nor do I need the money from things Daisy left behind."

Sailor couldn't help but gape at Ella. She figured you could always use money, especially when it was handed to you on a silver platter.

Seeing her discomfort, Ella looked away. She made a wide sweep with her hand and softly said, "The value we place on things can never take the place of the relationship we have with their owner. Daisy enjoyed collecting; I appreciate a more sedate look for my home. She knew that, but I'm also sure she knew me well enough to know that I will find a suitable place for everything she so lovingly chose for her home."

Ella motioned for Sailor to follow her and said, "Let's explore."

An hour later, Ella and Sailor sank into the cushions of the wicker sofa on the closed porch at the rear of the house. Sailor poured water into their glasses from the crystal pitcher they'd found in the kitchen cabinet. Taking a satisfying swallow of the refreshing drink she looked outside to where the recently mowed lawn divided numerous gardens. An assortment of plants, many of them in full bloom made the backyard a gardener's paradise. She marveled at the pristine condition of the house and its grounds. Earlier she had mentioned this to Ella and she had told her Daisy had retained a housekeeper and a gardener who had agreed to continue their tenure until the house was sold.

Nestled against the back of the sofa, Sailor decided to ask the question that had stayed on her mind since the morning drive to Douglas Landing. Not daring to look into Ella's wise eyes, Sailor continued to gaze at the backyard gardens and said, "Why do you and Elizabeth think I have unresolved issues?"

Ella heard the hurt of a small child's voice. She didn't answer right away. The silence was palpable as Ella waited on God's leading. Ella knew this could be a turning point in the life of one of God's children. She wanted to be sure the answer she gave was straight from the throne room of heaven.

Then ever so gently, she said, "Sailor, think about all of Daisy's possessions we have looked at today. To me, they are much the same because I don't know the true value of each item. But, you my dear do know the value because you possess knowledge that I don't have to evaluate antiques. Sometimes people will not see the value in another person and will let that cause him or her to devalue that person. As horrible as this is, it can never take away the true value God placed in each of us. When you see yourself through His eyes you will overcome the unresolved conflict that someone has thoughtlessly placed on you."

Ella graciously walked away, giving Sailor space. She clutched the chilled glass in her hand. She heard the clink of the ice touch the side of the glass and break into tiny slivers. At the same time she felt warmth melt some of the coldness that had frozen her heart.

Panic gripped her. What in the world was happening? First, Alex declares his love, then she feels the need to talk to God and now a stranger is reading her mind. Did Ella somehow know her hidden secret? Impossible . . . she'd just met her. She couldn't know. Thomasville, Georgia was a long ways from Mandeville, Louisiana. Her secret was safe as long as she kept it buried deep inside where no one could see the ugliness of the real Sailor Corbin.

7

The distant sound of the waves blended with the hum of the traffic as Sailor drove on the narrow two-lane road. From the corner of her eye she could see Ella sitting beside her in the car, her head turned towards the window.

Sailor had avoided further conversation about Ella's insight into her private thoughts, choosing to let sleeping dogs lie rather than try to explain her reaction to the reference of unresolved issues.

As the road turned inland, Sailor slowed the car, retracing their earlier drive through the small coastal communities. Several miles passed before Ella spoke. "It felt very strange to plunder through Daisy's belongings."

Sailor looked at Ella and caught her staring at her. Not past her or through her, but right straight at her.

Sailor squirmed and ran her fingers around the smooth surface of the steering wheel.

"I think God is plundering around in my belongings too."

When Ella didn't respond, Sailor glanced in the rear-view mirror and turned the signal before she slowed and pulled into the exit for the public strip of beach in Carrabelle. She waited until a group of men loaded with fishing gear passed in front of her car, and then parked the car next to the picnic tables. Lots of folks strolled along the surf. A few were clustered underneath red and yellow striped beach umbrellas that fluttered in the breeze blowing from the Gulf.

Sailor sat with her hands on the steering wheel, her eyes were red-rimmed but dry. She looked at the serene scenery in front of her and wished with all her heart she could make the events of yesteryear disappear like the white foam topping the waves and then sucked into oblivion by the ebb and flow of the tides.

"I'm alright now," Sailor whispered. But, Ella knew better. She didn't look alright. Ella had lived long enough to read body language and Sailor's was screaming, help!

"Please, Sailor. Let me help you," Ella encouraged.

Sailor turned to Ella, still gripping the steering wheel so tightly her knuckles were milky white in the waning sunlight. Her ebony eyes were deep pools of midnight misery that reached down into Ella's soul. All the maternal instincts rose inside Ella and she bonded with Sailor much like a mother bonds with her child at birth. The yearning to erase the hurt in Sailor's eyes was so strong Ella reached out and laid her hand on Sailor's shoulder. Her blue-veined hands with their crepe-paper thin skin caressed her with gentle strokes.

When Ella felt some of the tension leave Sailor she said, "My sweet girl, whatever has caused you so much pain needs to be released into God's care. We are not made to carry so heavy a burden."

Sailor's eyes filled with tears. "I'm so sorry for being such a baby. I don't know what to do. All of a sudden it's like my life is exposed for everyone to see and I don't seem to have any control over my life anymore."

"I want you to know, I'm here for you. I believe God orchestrates our comings and goings and He knows right where we are at this precise moment."

She cupped Sailor's chin with her hand, lifting her head until their eyes were even. She brushed a strand of hair out of her eyes and said, "Do you want to tell me what is causing you so much pain?"

. . .

Briefly, Sailor told Ella about the trepidation she was feeling about her relationship with Alex. She also told her about the sudden desire to talk with God, but she never broached the root of the sadness that hung to her much like a thick fog on a cold winter night. Even though the older woman was nothing but kindness itself, Sailor could not form the words to expose the abuse that still held her in its gripe of secrecy.

The remainder of the drive to Thomasville was nice with each of them silently agreeing to move away from the emotional encounter and concentrate on more pleasant things. They discussed the best way to handle the sale of Daisy's house and the vast array of valuable assets she'd left behind at her death. Sailor promised to be available to drive Ella to Douglas Landing if she needed to return.

By the time they arrived at Ella's house Sailor could see the fatigue in the elderly woman's eyes. She parked the car and went around opening the car door. Holding Ella's arm to give her support, Sailor walked with her to the house.

Elizabeth heard them drive up and opened the door. She stood in the doorway, the lamp light in the room casting shadows around her plump body. Sailor declined the invitation to come inside saying it was late and she needed to get home. The truth was, she was afraid Elizabeth would pick up where

Ella had left off and she just wasn't ready to face her demons again tonight.

An hour later she had finished her nightly rituals and crawled into Grandmere Elise's feather bed hoping with all her heart she would have a dreamless night of rest.

8

Sailor had been dreading this moment. Since she'd arrived at work she'd tried to ignore most of the phone calls by letting them go straight to voice mail. She scooted to the edge of her seat and scowled through the incoming calls half-way dreading yet curious to see if Alex had called. He had. She stared at the number; her finger paused above the playback key.

She wasn't surprised he'd called. Sailor was sure he'd already figured out she was trying to avoid talking with him. Alex would never impose on her time. He was too polite to be overbearing. She knew he would overlook her slight, giving her the benefit of being busy with work or absorbed in a new project.

Her prayer for a dreamless night had been ignored by God. Instead, she'd awakened around five-thirty feeling wrung out from a fitful night of being chased by unseen assailants. Snatches of conversation echoed around her in the eerie grayness of the Louisiana woods. It was a nightmare that had played out in her mind for years, but each time it came her soul was damaged just a little bit more.

Now, she sat at her desk, her eyes shadowed by dark circles the careful application of make-up this morning could not erase. For a moment, Sailor closed her eyes.

After an intense internal struggle, she punched the key to return Alex's call. She listened to the familiar sound of the church bells of his ringtone. It made her smile, but the smile quickly turned into a frown when she heard his voice say, "Your call is important to me and I'll get back with you as soon as possible."

"Rats. I can't do anything right today," Sailor complained. "Might as well go home and crawl back in bed to see if my demons are still hanging out there."

She returned the half-dozen calls and recorded a new message that she and Daughtry were out of the office for the rest of the day. It wouldn't cause a hardship for their clientele who knew they would get a callback if something needed to be attended quickly.

On the trip home, Sailor called Vickie to invite her over for supper. She accepted. The thought of her best friend coming to see her soothed the uneasiness lurking inside her chest.

She slowed the car behind a long line of traffic as cars pulled into the turn lane for the Walmart close to her townhouse. Sailor glanced into the rearview mirror and eased over into the turn lane. She wanted to make a pot of chili and grilled cheese sandwiches for supper and remembered she was out of chili powder and sliced cheese. Cooking was her way of unwinding and chili and grilled cheese was at the top of her comfort-food list. Plus, comfort food was always better when shared with a friend. She realized she needed both tonight.

Bypassing the shopping carts she collected what she needed and headed to the self-check aisle. She scanned the items, paid, put her stuff in a plastic bag and was out the door without having to speak to a single person.

Mumbling, she slid into the car, berating herself for being such a crabapple. She was usually a very positive, upbeat person. Somehow the past days had taken a toll on her emotions and it was for sure she would have to get a handle on what had thrown her off kilter. But, not tonight she thought as she left the Walmart parking lot and drove the couple of miles to her home.

. . .

Sailor sautéed the ground beef, and then added salt and chopped onions. The aroma of the meat intensified as she slowly stirred until it was nice and brown before adding a can of diced tomatoes, dark-red kidney beans and chili powder. Turning the burner to low she covered the pot and allowed it to cook for the next thirty minutes. During that time she changed into shorts and a sleeveless shirt and was on the way to the kitchen to gather the bread, cheese, butter and the flat skillet when she heard Vickie calling her name at the front door.

She hurried to open the door and was enveloped in a bear hug when Vickie grabbed her almost squeezing the breath out of her lungs.

Eyes dancing with excitement, Vickie released her long enough to say, "Yum, something smells delicious! I can't wait to tell you what happened today!"

Used to Vickie's ever present sense of joy, Sailor laughed and said, "Did your new boyfriend propose?"

Vickie's hazel eyes grew round. "Who told you? Wait, that's impossible, I haven't told anyone."

Sailor took a step backwards. "Wait a minute . . . I was kidding . . . whoa . . . are you serious?"

For the first time all day Sailor felt happy, and her smile widened. She stared at Vickie who was standing there with a silly grin on her face, shaking her head up and down like a bobble-head doll.

Still wearing the grin, Vickie swept into the room as if she was floating on air and turned to look at Sailor.

"Stop right there," Sailor commanded. She wiggled her hands in the air. "Are you telling me Mason Butler, the movie producer you met less than a month ago asked you to marry him?"

Vickie took up the bobble-head motion again and held her left hand under Sailor's nose. A huge square-cut diamond set on her ring finger, sparkling with blue streaks of fire as the overhead light caught its beauty.

"Oh my word. That's an engagement ring. A big, diamond engagement ring!"

Vickie studied Sailor, her face expressionless, but it didn't last but a moment. Words bubbled from her as she chattered excitedly about the lunch date with Mason near the site of Lake Jackson where his movie company planned to film.

Not understanding a word of the hurried explanation, Sailor stopped her mid-sentence, took her hand and said, "Hold that thought. Come with me to the kitchen so I can check to make sure the chili is not sticking to the bottom of the pot."

Vickie giggled and then obediently followed Sailor into the kitchen.

"Sit," Sailor said. Vickie sat. She watched Sailor stir the chili and then turn off the burner underneath the pot.

Sailor took a deep breath as she settled in the chair across from Vickie. "Now, tell me everything. Don't leave out a single detail."

At seven o'clock they were finishing up their second helping of chili and saltines after foregoing the grilled cheese sandwiches because Sailor was too involved in the tale of love that Vickie was weaving.

Vickie glowed with the bloom of love as she told Sailor that Mason was everything she'd prayed for. He was a believer, he was a true gentleman and he loved children. But most of all, he loved her, and had proven it time and again in the past month as they'd spent time together getting to know each other.

"How could I not know this was happening to my best friend?"

"Aw, Sailor, I'm sorry you feel left out. You were busy and it all happened so quickly. But, now I need you more than ever. We have a wedding to plan."

A shaky sigh leaked from Sailor's throat. "You don't owe me an apology. If I hadn't been so caught up in my own emotional junk, I would have been a better friend and seen what was happening."

Vickie felt the shift in the conversation and reached out to lay a comforting hand on Sailor's arm. She noticed the brightness of unshed tears in Sailor's ebony eyes. The pain evident in the spoken words drew Vickie away from talk of love and weddings as she softly asked Sailor, "Can you share this heavy burden with your friend or do I need to pretend I can't see your hurt and move on to another subject?"

Sailor broke. The tears flowed down her cheeks as she laid her head against her friend's chest. Vickie held her without uttering a word.

When she thought Sailor could speak she gently said, "Sailor, I was raised to believe that God can solve any problem if we ask for His help. Obviously there is something in your life that is causing you a great deal of pain. It's up to you whether you want God's help or not. I could ask for you, but God would prefer you go to Him."

With her dark eyes washed shiny from the tears, Sailor looked at Vickie and said, "That's the problem. I don't have one problem; I have an accumulation of problems that have multiplied over the years. I don't get it. You are so sure of your faith and you're so sure that Mason loves you that you are willing to commit to a life with him. I am stumbling around like a toddler afraid to take a single step in any direction for fear I'll make the wrong choice."

Vickie chuckled. "Ha, let me tell you about wrong choices, that is if you have the rest of the night to listen. Humans do dumb things, but always have the ability to dust themselves off and move away from the bad choices and start over. It's the starting over that trip so many of us up. We get stuck in the mud of a bad choice and guilt piles mud on top of us until we are mired so deep it feels like quicksand is stifling the life out of us. That's when we cry out to God for help and He provides a way of escape when there doesn't seem to be a way."

She listened to her friend express her faith in God, and marveled that it could be as simple as believing He would do the same for her if she put her trust in Him.

"I want to believe, Vickie, but my mind refuses to cooperate with what my heart is saying," Sailor said.

9

There were times life confounded Sailor. She'd slept soundly all night and had awakened refreshed.

Stretching her arms high above her head she lay in the softness of her Grandmere's bed recalling last night's conversation with Vickie. They'd been friends for years, but Sailor had always guarded her secret from everyone, even her best friend. That is, until last night.

She wasn't sure what had prompted her to change her mind. Perhaps it was seeing the happiness shining in Vickie's eyes as she told her of her engagement to Mason, or maybe it was the time spent with Ella yesterday.

Whatever the reason, Sailor had bared her soul last night. And, today she was thankful.

Her eyes misted with tears as she remember the moment she'd whispered the ugly words, "I was raped."

She didn't know what reaction she expected from her friend, but Vickie did what any person with an ounce of human kindness would do. She'd folded Sailor in her arms and wept with her just as if the horrible act was carried out on her own body. The empathy she'd shared with her should have been enough to purge the darkness of the heinous assault and move pass the prison of blaming herself. But, knowing the facts of the truth doesn't always bring immediate freedom. Still, it had given Sailor hope that someday the tentacles of self-doubt could be forever erased.

Sunshine trailed across the ivory coverlet on her bed. Her fingers traced its path leading up to her chest. Could this be the beginning of a new phase in her life? One filled with light instead of the darkness that had always hovered on the edges of her days. She knew life was complicated, but the strength she'd gained from last night's conversation with Vickie gave her reason to believe there were new beginnings. Vickie said each day was a gift, to be opened with anticipation and joy. Lord knows she wanted to believe her friend was right,

She glanced at the clock and sat up with a start. Nine o'clock! She needed to get to work!

Jumping out of bed Sailor's feet hit the floor with a thud before she realized today was Saturday.

Muttering, she ambled into the kitchen at a slower pace. Slipping a bottle of chilled water from the fridge and a handful of green grapes, she picked up the TV remote and scrolled to WCTV Ch.6. Munching the grapes she listened to the latest poll numbers of the presidential race. Just like yesterday, Donald Trump and Hillary Clinton were the front runners. Not one to linger over politics, Sailor clicked the TV off and took a thirsty swallow of cool water.

Her cell phone sounded inside her purse where she placed it on the bar last night. It was Alex. Her breath caught in her throat. Clearing her throat, she answered the call.

"Alex, it's good to hear from you."

His deep voice brought a tingle of longing.

"Good morning, Sailor. How's my best girl?"

She grinned and her heart went pitter-pat. "Best girl, huh, maybe I need to ask how many girls you are courting."

He heard the playful humor in her voice and said, "Oh, let me see there's Connie and Bettie . . . and Susie . . ."

Alex noticed the silence and quickly backtracked. "I'm teasing, Sailor. There isn't anyone but you."

She remembered the confidence that Vickie had shown last night as she'd talked about Mason and how sure she was that he was the one man in the world that God had created just for her.

The memory sparked a confidence in Sailor and she declared, "Alex, may I ask a favor?"

"Of course, you may ask me anything."

She fought to keep the tremble out of her voice, determined to face her demons with her head held high.

Alex had offered her his love, but along with that came the responsibility to love the people of his church. Was she brave enough to face rejection if they couldn't accept her nationality?

They'd been more than cordial when she had met some of them at Colton and Loren's wedding held in their church last year, but this was entirely different. If her instinct could be trusted she was sure Alex was leading up to a marriage proposal and that was way more than being accepted as a member of a wedding party.

Alex was quiet. She could hear his light breathing and she pictured him. A strong man who worked out because he believed God made us to care for our bodies by keeping them healthy, dark brown hair cut short but with enough curl that it refused to lay flat, eyes as blue and guileless as a newborn and a smile that could calm anyone who came within seeing distance.

When she spoke again she was talking from her heart. "Alex, there's a lot going on inside me right now and I'm not sure just how much I can share with you but, if the invitation is still open for me to come visit you, I'd like to accept."

Sailor heard a loud bang on the phone when Alex pumped his arms in the air and dropped his cell phone to the floor. She stared at her phone wondering what had caused the loud commotion, until she heard Alex say, "Sorry about that. I dropped my phone. Uh, now, did I hear you say you would like to come for a visit?"

Confidence rose inside her. "Yes, I would love to spend some time with you and get to know the people who are a part of your life."

He didn't reply for a moment and her momentary confidence fled. "Alex, did I say the wrong thing?"

"Lord, no, you said the right thing and you've just made me the happiest man in Georgia. I can't wait to see you."

She spotted movement outside her kitchen window and glanced towards it. The door was open and Vickie stepped into the house. She wore a short-sleeved shirt and jeans. Instead of closed shoes, she had on open-toed sandals. Her hair fell in loose waves of dark and light, her expression happy.

Closing the door, Vickie waited until she heard Sailor say goodbye and laid her cell phone on the kitchen bar.

"What are you doing up so early?"

"Couldn't sleep. My mind is racing in a dozen directions, so I figured I might as well follow through on a couple of them."

Sailor eyed her. "I woke early too. Alex called."

Vickie listened intently. Her gaze never left Sailor's face.

"So, are you okay," she asked quietly.

She nodded. "I am more than okay. I told Alex I would come to Peron for a visit."

Vickie smiled and walked closer to give Sailor a hug.

Vickie understood what a huge step this was for Sailor. They both knew it could be a turning point. Where it would lead was entirely up to Sailor, but Vickie was confident she had found her starting point for a new life that would involve a certain Georgia preacher.

Vickie held her at arm's length and grinned. "I feel a romance in the making. Get dressed; we're going wedding gown shopping!"

A panic-struck look glazed Sailor's eyes. Vickie saw the look and laughed. "Not for you silly, for me!"

10

The Wedding Boutique in downtown Tallahassee was a combination of satin, sequins and excited brides-to-be chattering. They rushed to the fitting rooms with arms loaded with yards of white perfection.

Sailor and Vickie stood in the center of the boutique and watched the faces of the girls as they disappeared into the fitting rooms. Moments later they heard a squeal of joy that brought total silence to the room as one of the brides rushed out in a gorgeous gown and said, "This is the one!"

Sailor eyed her friend with speculation. Vickie's perfectly arched eyebrows rose as a beautiful lady wove her way through the crowd to stand in front of them with her hand extended in welcome.

Pleased to be welcomed in such a warm manner, Sailor and Vickie reached for the lady's hand simultaneously. She laughed softly and took their hands in hers.

"Come in, please. I'm Mia, and we're so pleased you've chosen to visit our boutique today. How may I assist you?"

Vickie's expressive hazel eyes glistened with joy. "I've come to choose my wedding dress."

"Wonderful." Mia swept her hand towards the multiple racks of gowns. "As you can see, we have a large selection to fit any wedding theme you choose."

She glanced at Sailor, and then back at Mia. "A small, intimate wedding is what we want in the middle of a flower garden surrounded with the beauty of God's nature." Seeing their interest she went on, "I dream of a dress that catches the gentle breeze and I become one with all creation as I move down a flower-strewn path towards Mason."

Mia laid her hand on her chest and sighed. "Oh my darling girl, I have the most wondrous gown just for you. Follow me. I know you'll love it," she gushed.

Vickie's first glimpse of the gown brought tears of overwhelming joy. She was speechless. Mia was right, it was her dream gown.

When Mia lifted the soft confection of beauty and laid it over Vickie's outstretched arms it gently swayed, falling in silky white softness as perfect as a summer cloud.

As Sailor watched her friend gush over finding her dream wedding dress, something akin to the feeling you get when you take a sip of hot chocolate during the coldest night of the year settled inside her. It soothed her. It made her dream of the possibility of being a bride and finding the ideal dress to express who she was as she walked down the aisle to become one with the love of her life.

The moment passed as swiftly as it had come when cruel voices of accusations in her head taunted her, reminding her that she would never be worthy to wear white or come to her husband unsoiled. Her warm dream faded. No matter how she tried to erase the past it clung to her like the stench of decaying garbage, always crushing her dream and making her feel worthless.

Sailor adjusted the mask she'd worn for most of her life. She smiled, agreeing with Vickie that she'd found the gown that would knock Mason off his feet.

But, underneath the guise, Sailor's past had once again managed to dim the dream of marriage and a family even though she'd felt so hopeful this morning when she'd agreed to visit Alex. Now, she wasn't so sure she could follow through on her plan.

11

A honeybee orchestra serenaded the pink azaleas as Sailor followed Mason and Vickie to the Secret Garden at MaClay State Park. A thick hedge of greenery formed a trellis at the entry giving it a mysterious invitation that drew visitors inside.

A swirl of emotions welled up in Sailor as she watched Mason embrace Vickie. They smiled at each other, love so evident in their eyes that Sailor felt like an intruder in such an intimate moment. At the same time she couldn't help the longing to see Alex as she imagined what it must feel like to plan your wedding day together.

"Wow . . . just wow." Vickie let the words escape in a rushed exhale. The garden was more than she'd expected. "I can't believe I've lived in

Tallahassee over ten years and never visited this place. It's gorgeous," Vickie exclaimed as she swept her arms wide in an effort to embrace the beauty surrounding them. She slowly turned to look at the vibrant Azalea and Camilla blooms that filled the garden with colorful beauty. A reflection pool in the distance caught the images in the shimmering clear water doubling nature's bounty.

Sailor's breath caught in her throat. Her longing to see Alex increased.

Vickie grabbed her hand and drew her closer. "It's perfect. I love everything about this place."

Mason laid his cheek against the top of Vickie's head and said, "I agree, this is the place. What about you, Sailor, agree . . . disagree?"

She released her breath and grinned. "Agree."

Mason wrapped his arms around Vickie and Sailor was moved to be witness to one of God's greatest gifts. True love did exist, and if she could be totally honest with herself she knew Alex was the one for her. The only thing standing in the way was all the hang-ups she'd allowed to hold her in bondage. Guilt, low-esteem, unworthiness . . . the list was endless. Somehow she had to break free.

12

Pastor Alex Collins was driving out of town on that sunny afternoon. Navigating the car slowly down the country road he took in the beauty of North Georgia. Nature was at its best this time of year as life rose from its resting place to begin anew. A couple of brown rabbits with their long ears held at attention and white cotton tails to the ground stood like sentinels at the side of the road. Their button noses twitched with curiosity causing him to laugh out loud.

He wished Sailor could share the moment with him. The thought tugged at him, and her beautiful face materialized in his mind. With each passing day he was more certain she was the woman God had created to be his wife. So far, he had managed to move slowly not wanting to drive her away by his declaration of love, but somehow, during his prayer time lately he'd felt an urgency that maybe Sailor was ready to hear his heart's message. Many times he'd asked God to move mountains in other people's lives and he'd seen the impossible happen. If God could answer his prayers for others, surely He'd answer Alex's prayer for himself.

"God, You know my heart's desire is to do Your will. I've waited patiently for you to send me the one who would complete my life. As a pastor, I know the importance of choosing well, so let me be led by my spirit and not by my emotions, I pray in Jesus Name."

No sooner had he whispered amen his cell phone rang. Alex pulled to the side of the road to answer. It was Sailor. He smiled as he connected and said, "Hello."

"Alex, I just wanted to call and invite you to Mason and Vickie's wedding. They aren't sending out invitations. It will be a very small gathering of friends and family, but . . . well; I just wanted you to be here."

He recognized the peace that came with answered prayer. God was putting the pieces of their lives together. His job was to follow God's gentle leading by not taking matters in his own hands.

Easier said than done he mumbled under his breath as he said, "Thank you, Sailor. I'll be there."

13

Saturday morning Sailor rinsed the last of her breakfast dishes and left them to air-dry. She enjoyed the convenience of the dishwasher when company came to eat, but when it was just her she made quick work of the job by hand-washing the few dishes she'd used. Besides that, the simple chore reminded her of time spent at her grandmother's house. They'd used the time together for so much more than cleaning the kitchen. It was during those times that Sailor learned about her family's history.

Sailor remembered her heart would pound with anticipation as Grandmere Elise filled the sink with hot water and the bubbly suds would rise to the top of the sink covering the dishes with glistening mounds of soap. She'd bounce from one foot to the other foot until Grandmere would say, "Sailor, you come from a long line of strong women. Women who faced hardship but didn't let it determine their destiny. No sir, we learned early in life that we are the master of our destiny and it's our choices that determine our final destination."

Grandmere's beautiful almond-shaped eyes as dark as the deep water of the Louisiana bayou would pierce deep into Sailor's eyes and she'd ask, "Do you understand, Sailor?"

The memory was so real Sailor's throat felt tight with sadness as the echo of the question lingered in the kitchen. Did she truly believe Grandmere? Was she the master of her destiny?

She leaned against the door frame as another memory flooded her mind. Her breath caught in her throat. She cried out in pain as spectral images of hands grabbed at her, wiping away her innocence, her dignity, forcing her in a direction she knew would alter her life as she lay helpless to prevent its ugliness.

Her knees buckled under the weight of her sorrow and she slid to the floor. "Dear God, please take this from me. I can't bear it anymore," she sobbed.

Tears ran down her face, blurring the brightness of the early morning sun as she cried for the lost child inside her. She believed she'd broken her Daddy and Mama's heart from the look of horror on their faces when she'd ran inside the house. Her clothes were ripped and her body caked with mud, mingled with the blood running down her legs to puddle on the clean floor. Her parents had always protected her with their unconditional love, but, that day there was a bridge between them as she tried to explain what had happened to her. Instead of wrapping their arms around her they had stood at a distance. Her Daddy's words nailed the coffin shut when he told her it was over, and she was to pretend it never happened.

He had turned his back to her and Mama led her from the room. She had gathered clean clothes for her, filled the tub with hot water and told her to take a bath. When she'd come into her room, Mama was there.

Mama kissed her goodnight and whispered, "I'm so sorry, Sailor. Your Daddy knows what's best. He'll take care of you. No one ever has to know."

Sailor lifted her head. Sorrow filled her heart. True to Daddy and Mama's words, he had taken care of her physically, and as far as she knew no one ever learned their family secret.

But, the secret had come with a high price. She had paid daily with the load of guilt that held her emotions in prison. By the time she'd become an adult she knew in her heart that they were only trying to protect her from the shame associated with the public scrutiny of rape victims.

To make up for what she thought was her failure at being good, she'd became the perfect child, who made straight A's all through school and college, but underneath the façade of perfection she never got pass the assault that robbed her of her most precious gift. No matter how successful, how polished she was on the outside. Sailor always felt soiled on the inside.

Her Grandmere's words came to her. How had she explained it? "It's God who forgives, God who loves. Just be still and let Him do that."

"I'm sorry, God, I don't know how to be still. I don't know how to hear You."

A dull, rushing noise filled her head as deep sorrow took hold. Her body ached. Tears burned her eyes, and a voiceless cry scraped her throat raw.

At last she knew – this was being still, with nowhere else to turn to, but would God really listen?

14

Sailor walked through the flower trellis entrance of the secret garden in McClay State Park. She paused long enough to look at Alex. A smile curled the corners of his mouth that stretched to a full grin when his sky-blue eyes connected with Sailor's midnight eyes. Her heart went *thurumpt* inside her chest as she held his gaze long enough to feel the impact of the message of love he sent clear down to her toes.

"Move it, Sailor," Vickie said into her ear with a giggle.

Her words penetrated the magical glow of awareness Sailor was feeling as she broke Alex's ardent stare and slowly moved one foot in front of the other towards the beautifully decorated portable stage where Mason, his friend Trevor and Alex waited.

She was thrilled that Vickie and Mason had chosen to include Alex in their special day. He'd accepted their invitation to perform the nuptials and had driven to Tallahassee a few days early to counsel with the couple before their wedding day. Vickie had shared the serious tone Alex had used as he'd explained how God looked at marriage. She'd thought of the things Vickie had recounted and once again wondered if she'd ever get to the place where she felt worthy enough to share her life, mind, body and soul with another human being. She knew her heart melted every time she was around Alex, but her mind would override the emotion casting doubt about a future with him. She was torn as the battle to find peace of mind raged inside her, creating a barrier that she'd been unable to cross.

A thundering round of applause brought Sailor back to the present, and she realized her musing had caused here to miss the entire ceremony. She saw Alex place his hands on Vickie and Mason's shoulders as they continued to keep their lips locked in a post-ceremony kiss. He laughed and politely cleared his throat before saying, "Uh, folks I'll introduce the happy couple just as soon as they finish attending to important business."

"Alex," Sailor whispered as she turned to face him. He shrugged his shoulders and Sailor felt warmth spread inside her as she got a glimpse of a playful side of his personality. He was unlike any pastor she'd ever known, always surprising her by acting so down to earth instead of all high and mighty like someone who thought they never had to ask God for forgiveness.

Much to the amusement of everyone, Mason and Vickie grabbed hands and waltzed off the stage with all the aplomb of a scene straight out of a 30's movie drama. Trevor followed suit by taking Sailor's hand and walking in like-manner. Sailor didn't need to turn around to know that Alex was following close behind her. When he was near, her senses were so attuned to his presence she could literally feel his eyes watching her and smell the spicy scent from his body wrapping around her in a gentle hug.

• • •

Alex got to his feet and stretched his hand to Sailor in a wordless invitation. She blinked, surprised at the invitation to dance. The stars illuminated the dance floor adding a soft glow making the open space intimate.

They crossed the floor hand in hand and found space on the dance floor just as the band swung into a tune from the past. Alex drew Sailor close. She tipped her face and smiled. She decided conversation was overrated when you were able to communicate on a much closer level without words.

His hazy blue eyes spoke volumes in the moonlight and she responded by laying her head against his chest. His hand tightened on her waist. She felt secure snuggled close to the solid strength of his body.

Was this what it felt like to love someone? This unexplainable feeling of rightness, without the threat of being used and then tossed away was entirely foreign to Sailor. She'd never allowed herself to be close to a man other than her dad and brother since she was twelve years old.

It was a sobering thought, but somehow it felt right. Sailor felt the broken pieces of her self-esteem begin to heal as Alex held her ever so lovingly while they swayed to the music of one of the most famous of Elvis Presley's songs, Love Me Tender.

15

The sunlight was peeking through the window when Sailor awakened. She glanced at the clock on the bedside table. It was seven o'clock. Although she'd forgotten to set her alarm, her internal clock woke her at the usual time she got up each morning. Stifling a huge yawn, Sailor wiggled her toes underneath the cool sheets and then let her thoughts drift to Mason and Vickie's wedding yesterday.

She closed her eyes and remembered the moment she'd walked into the garden and saw Alex. In a second's time she'd taken in his tall, clean-cut body. He reminded Sailor of a magazine cover advertising how to dress for success in his dove-grey suit and white shirt set off by a spunky red-polka-dot bowtie.

Remembering the way his eyes had connected with hers brought a shiver of delight to her body, but the feeling was short-lived. Whereas she'd felt loved moments before, the feeling of worthlessness rolled over her, dragging her to a new depth of despair. She massaged her temples, eyes shut. The tight band behind her eyes held her in its grip. Her shoulders rose and fell against the bed as she attempted to escape the torture.

Her legs wobbled like jelly as she finally rolled from the bed and fell to her knees on the floor. Almost choking on the words she cried, "Dear God, help me."

The memory jumped at her again, the one when she was twelve walking home from school. She shivered as the feel of icy rain traced the tears on her face while she lay helpless at the mercy of those who committed unspeakable acts against her mind, body and soul. Her heart pounded in her chest, throat, and ears. Shame washed over her in waves threatening to drown her. She reached for the edge of the bed using it as an anchor to keep from falling on the floor. Desperate, Sailor shouted at God, *"You let this happen to me!"*

She spun around and laid her head against the bed, appalled that she had spoken her thoughts aloud. Her body shook as she waited for God to strike her dead for voicing her pain. Moments passed, and she realized the only sound she heard was the unsteady breath from her own body. She focused on the sound. And then so faint she almost missed it, she heard a gentle whisper inside her spirit, "You know I'm closer to you than the air you breathe."

Sailor coiled into the fetal position and let the tears flow. "I'm so sorry, God, I have been so angry with You. Please help me find the key to unlock this prison of guilt I've lived in for so long"

The room filled with warmth, not the kind that comes from the sun. Sailor's anxieties lessened. She breathed in the air around her and marveled that God would speak to her. Sitting straighter, she bravely asked God to allow her time before they discussed the other issues. She knew forgiveness towards the boys that had raped her had to be faced, but she just wasn't capable of dealing with its ugliness yet.

Still shaky, she stood and gathered every bit of faith and courage she could muster. She wanted to attend church . . . no, she needed to attend church.

Rushing to get ready, she dressed in a summery floral dress in shades of pastel blue, and brushed her hair, leaving it loose to flow down her back in natural curls.

If she hurried she could make it in time for the morning worship service. Grabbing her purse on the way to the door, she was startled when it opened from the outside and she came face to face with her brother Daughtry.

"Whoa, you scared the daylight out of me."

Daughtry laughed and gave her a quick hug. "Oops, sorry, I got in late last night so I didn't call." He backed up and whistled. "Where are you going all dressed up on a Sunday morning?"

A smile spread across her face and her dark eyes sparkled. "I'm on the way to church. You want to come?"

He raised his chin. "Did I hear right, you're going to church? That's not your usual Sunday morning routine. Should I be worried that someone has taken over my sister's body?"

Sailor stood still for a long moment before speaking. "I will tell you all about it later, but I had an up close and personal encounter with God this morning, so yes, I'm going to honor His day by attending church. Would you like to come with me?" she asked hopefully.

He tilted his head and then gave her half a nod. "Yes, matter of fact; I'd love to attend church with you. It appears God has been busy talking to the Corbin siblings this week. I have some interesting news to share with you."

16

Sailor bent over in front of the oven and pulled out a baking sheet of fresh hot sugar cookies.

Hymns flowed in her mind, one after another like the waves rolling toward the shore. "Amazing Grace" "Blessed Assurance" "How great Thou Art" One . . . after . . . another. Verse upon verse. Crescendo upon crescendo.

Chasing away the guilt.

There were so many reasons for the guilt, not the least of which was her neglect to include God in her life. She blamed her wounded heart for her behavior. No, the truth was she blamed God for her behavior. The encounter with God this morning burned like a hot fire under her, forcing her to see things differently, to react differently.

The words Pastor Kole had spoken at church this morning encouraged her to recognize she was in a battle to regain the part of her life that had been stolen. Sailor thought he was looking straight at her when he said, "God loves all His children." Amazingly, she was starting to believe it was true.

And then, out of nowhere the familiar darkness eddied around her like a whirlpool, threatening to swamp any trace of well-being.

"No," she shouted to the pressure to give in to the enemy who'd held her captive for so long.

With renewed determination, Sailor filled the pastry tool with bright yellow icing and methodically drew smiley faces on each of the cookies. As she worked she listened to the inner voice that echoed the pastor's words from this morning. He'd said that guilt was much like a minefield and if a person tried to navigate their steps without God's help they would continually step on areas that were sure to blow up in their face.

She inspected the cookie. The wide smile she'd drawn was so cocky it brought a smile to her lips in spite of the seriousness of her internal conversation.

"Help me Lord. I admit I have been living in a minefield of guilt."

She began to sing the song they'd sang at church. "Leaning, leaning, safe and secure from all alarm. Leaning, leaning, leaning on the everlasting arms."

Sailor took a bite out of the cookie. What was it pastor said? The word hope glowed like a lighthouse beacon in her mind, beckoning her to leave the perilous waters of her past and row her boat of life towards its welcoming arms.

"Hope. I choose hope. I do. Hope is from You. Fear is not."

"Sailor."

She turned and saw Daughtry standing in the doorway of the kitchen. She'd been so absorbed in her conversation she hadn't heard the front door open. He grinned and stepped towards her. "Are you talking to yourself?"

"Me, myself, and I." She shrugged. "And God."

Daughtry walked across the room, his arms held wide. "Sounds like good company."

Sailor returned her brother's hug and said, "Yeah, I'm beginning to believe He's the best company in the world." She pointed to the chair. "Sit while I create a smiley face cookie for you."

He took the cookie she handed him and popped the entire morsel into his mouth. With one side of his jaw stuffed with cookies, he spoke out of the other side. "What were you and God talking about?"

She didn't respond for a few seconds. Did she dare approach the subject that had been taboo in her family for years?

Deciding it was now or never to allow God to direct her through the minefield of her past she looked directly at her brother and said, "Let me introduce myself. I'm Sailor Corbin and I just discovered Jesus likes me. As a matter of fact, he's crazy about me. Even when I'm not perfect He's willing to carry me through the rough places of my faults until I see my error and ask Him for forgiveness."

Daughtry didn't reply.

"Does that make sense to you?"

Silence.

She waited a long moment and then plunged ahead, surprising herself with her next words. "I forgive you, Daughtry."

She saw hurt flicker in his eyes. "What do you mean?"

She ignored the look of hurt and the hint of his self-righteous tone. "You never said a word about what those boys did to me. You were just like Mama and Daddy, pretending it never happened. But, it did and I needed you to be my big brother and to defend me."

107

A flush warmed his cheeks. She heard the sharp intake of his breath.

"I'm so sorry, Sailor. I thought you didn't want me to talk about it,"

The childlike hurt in her voice was his undoing when she whispered, "No one came to my rescue."

Tears welled in his eyes. "Oh my God, Sailor, I tried, I wanted to kill those boys. They were supposed to be my friends. You were spending the night with Grandmere and I overheard Dad and Mom talking about it. I went to get Dad's gun out of the locked gun case in the hall closet. I was so angry, I dropped the revolver and they heard me. Dad rushed out and grabbed the gun from me, demanding to know what was going on."

She blinked back tears.

It was time for the truth. Sailor placed a hand at her chest and prompted herself. No more straitjacket. No more binding myself.

"I thought you were all ashamed of me, that it was my fault it happened."

"No, Sailor, I never felt that way. I understand Dad and Mom thought they were protecting you by not letting it go public, but maybe we were wrong. Dad told me that he and Mom couldn't bear any more hurt and that if I killed those boys I would spend my life in prison. They said the best thing I could do was to go on as if nothing happened and that eventually we'd all put it in the past and move on with our lives."

She thought of her spontaneous songfest. Could she truly lean on the arms of God?

Wiping at the corner of her eye, she nodded.

"In a way Daddy was right, we did move on with our lives. We've kept up appearances, but, I'm afraid mine has all been on the outside. Inside I've never healed enough to let go of the hurt. But, maybe that is about to change. I'm beginning to understand that God has placed people in my path who have spoken self-worth to me when I could only see worthlessness. It wasn't your fault, no more than it was mine. I want to move pass that time in my life and you need to do the same"

As if a plug had been pulled from a tub filled with water, Daughtry's guilt drained from him.

Then he said, "Didn't you ever wonder why I switched schools in the middle of my senior year?"

Sailor nodded.

"Dad knew if he let me stay in the same school with those guys I'd eventually smash their faces in the ground."

Tenderness for her brother stirred inside her. Her brother loved her. He had tried to defend her.

Sailor asked the question that had haunted her mind for years.

"Do you know what happened to them?"

He rubbed his hand across his eyes. "You never heard?"

Sailor shook her head.

"It seems justice prevailed in spite of my failure to act in your defense. The night of graduation they were drinking and driving when they veered into the path of a semi-truck. There was barely enough left to identify them."

A shocked expression lined Sailor's face. All those years of living in fear, dreading that they would hunt her down like a cornered animal . . . wasted . . .wasted . . .

They were gone. They could never hurt her again. It was over.

. . .

Daughtry and Sailor finished decorating the last batch of sugar cookies thirty minutes later. During that time he told her about what was happening in South Dakota. The excitement in his tales of finding artifacts that had not seen the light of day in thousands of years erased every hint of their earlier conversation. His usual cool professional demeanor gave way to the little boy who'd overturned every rock in their Louisiana yard looking for prehistoric finds.

He was an expert in antiquities, so this discovery was more than he'd ever dreamed. He told Sailor the team originally hoped to find evidence of Native American civilization in the area, but this could be something totally different. A civilization undiscovered, lost in the eons of time. So far, the find was so unusual; no one had the answer for what they had found.

"So, I take it, you're going back."

Daughtry bobbed his head, a boyish grin stretching his mouth wide.

"Yeah, looks like you've got everything under control here."

"And . . . what are you not telling me?"

His grin got wider. "Well, bones are not the only thing I discovered in the wilds of South Dakota."

Sailor zoomed in on him and waited.

Daughtry squared his shoulders and said, "Her name is Abigail."

He laughed a deep belly laugh. "Your mouth is hanging open."

Sailor closed it.

17

The sun was going down as Sailor arrived at Ella's Thomasville home. She heard voices as she stepped onto the front porch that wrapped around the side of the lovely two-story home.

She recognized the women's voices and followed the sound to the rose garden at the side of the house. Gorgeous roses from the palest pinks to the deepest reds were just starting to bloom. Sailor stood still and closed her eye. She breathed in the fragrance that saturated the late afternoon air. It was heavenly.

Ella and Elizabeth were so engrossed in their perusal of the glorious array of color lit by the fading rays of the sun that they failed to see her approach. She stood silent, watching the elderly ladies chat as they tended the roses. Their friendship reminded her of the friendship she and Vickie shared. The only difference was their ages.

A movement in the sky caught Sailor's eyes as shafts of light streamed across the heavens like countless arms uplifted in praise. *Hallowed be Thy Name*. The prayer showered over her heart and quietness reigned supreme as she walked from the porch to speak to them. They were so intent in cutting a few blooms, that she softly called Ella's name for fear she'd startle her.

Ella glanced up and smiled. "Oh my, you've caught us dawdling in the garden when we should have been inside to give you a proper welcome at the door."

Elizabeth took the brilliant red rose Ella held and placed it along with several others in varying shades of rich color, in a basket looped on her arm.

"Not to worry, Ella. This is a perfect greeting place." Sailor said. "The fragrance, the color, the soft breeze causing the leaves to sway . . . it reminds me of Grandmere's gardens in Mandeville."

Two pairs of eyes, one a deep chocolate brown and the other a faded blue version of Texas Bluebonnets scrutinized Sailor. They had lived on God's green earth long enough to recognize a definite shift in the demeanor of the young lady God had sent to them. From the first they had seen beneath the confident shell Sailor wore, to the scared child who trusted no one. But, now she looked different. The exterior Sailor was still the beautiful professional picture of today's successful business woman dressed in a white silk blouse and ecru slacks, but the two prayer warriors saw more, they saw the inner spirit of Sailor that radiated a calm peacefulness only given by our Creator.

As if reading their thoughts, Sailor said, "Thank you for the supper invitation, I have so much to tell you."

Sailor reached out both hands to them and felt the firm, yet soft clasp of the women that she knew were about to become her confidants. She knew their walk with God would not allow them to sit in judgment, nor would they scold her for her resistance to God's gentle call. Whatever she chose to tell them tonight would never be shared with another human being, but would be lovingly placed at the feet of the One who loves us unconditionally.

. . .

The ride from Thomasville to Tallahassee seemed to drift by in a glow of contentment for Sailor. Some wordless notion stirred within, beguiling and fragrant like those sun-kissed roses she'd carried inside Ella's house. Tangled up in it was a pang of longing for the years she'd lived under such condemnation. But, those years were gone; the present was what counted now.

She thought about the past hour with Ella and Elizabeth. She'd thoroughly enjoyed the succulent chicken roasted to perfection with fresh rosemary seasoning, green beans and fruit salad. As they dined Ella and Elizabeth listened to her without interrupting. When she'd spoken the last horrible words, they'd bound the injury in encouraging words of love before sending her on her way. They'd wisely suggested she call her parents to extend her forgiveness towards them just as she had to her brother, Daughtry.

Ella told her we free ourselves when we offer forgiveness for the offenses others commit against us.

Determined to follow through on the advice given to her by Ella and Elizabeth she punched in the number connecting her to her parent's home phone as soon as she walked in her townhouse door. It rang, once, twice, three times as her sweaty hand tightly clutched the cell phone.

About to hang up, she heard her Daddy say, "Hello, Sailor. How nice to get a call from my favorite daughter."

She hesitated a moment, her pulse pounding in her throat. Drawing in a ragged breath, Sailor silently asked God for the right words to say.

"Daddy, would you please get Mama and then put us on the speaker phone. I need to talk with y'all about what happened to me when I was twelve.

Maurice felt regret grip his heart as he called out to Emilie to come into the room.

His hand covered the phone. He whispered, "Sailor is on the phone, she wants to talk with us about the day she was raped."

Her pale face aged before his eyes as she sank to a nearby chair. The day they'd prayed would never come had arrived, and they were no more ready for its arrival than the day their precious child had come home rain-drenched, covered with blood and dirt from an assault they were helpless to prevent.

18

Eight days had passed since the supper with Ella and Elizabeth. Sailor had spent the time trying to digest the enormous changes occurring since the Sunday she had come clean with God, so to speak. Her boldness in speaking to her parents and her brother about the day she was raped and the aftermath that followed still amazed her. The stone-heavy guilt no longer existed. The simple act of saying the words, *I forgive,* had released her in a way she'd never dreamed possible. The response she'd received from those she loved had bolstered her hurting soul, making her brave enough to embrace a future she'd never imagined was possible for her.

Ella's inquiry into her personal life when she told her she had unresolved issues and that she needed to deal with them had haunted her endlessly.

She'd asked Ella the night they had supper how she'd known about the tragedy of her childhood. Ella's compassionate eyes the color of rich chocolate had filled with tears. Tears flowed from her eyes as she brokenly told them the entire story of the day her charmed life had taken a downward spiral.

Sailor learned the value of prayer warriors like Ella and Elizabeth that night, ordinary people who are called by God to fight for the souls of hurting people, many of whom they'll never meet. Ella said God didn't reveal the source of Sailor's pain to them, only that she had needs way beyond anything a human could provide. So they prayed, *Your will be done in Sailor's life*. It was enough. They prayed and God answered.

Her thoughts were interrupted when the door opened and Daughtry walked out of his office where he'd been holed up for the better part of an hour. His usually neat black hair was divided into sections like corn rows. He continued to rake his slender fingers across the top of his head. Sailor smiled, amused at the sight of her handsome brother who seemed to be on the verge of a temper fit.

"Sailor, I'm out of here for the rest of the day. If Abbie calls, take a message."

Eyebrows lifted, Sailor asked, "Abbie who?"

The raking stopped. He turned at the door. "Ms. Abigail Callahan, who thinks she is the expert of all things created in the universe. The very same conniving female Abbie of the red hair and sea green eyes that is slowly sending me into oblivion with her demands, that's who."

He made a smirking face at her as he deliberately closed the door with a thud.

Sailor stood to see if she could halt his departure and then abruptly sat when the phone rang.

"Corbin Antiquities, Sailor Corbin speaking."

"Where is that bigoted pompous man?"

Sailor pulled the receiver from her ear, stared at it for a moment and then placed it to her head again. "Excuse me; you must have the wrong number. Goodbye."

"Nooo….don't hang up please . . . I'm sorry. I didn't mean to spout off at the mouth. That man brings out my Irish temper and makes me forget the good manners me Da raised me to have."

The brogue was so evident in the caller's voice that Sailor didn't need an introduction to say, "This has to be Abbie, am I correct?"

A more sedate tone answered her question. "You are correct. I would appreciate it if you would inform Dr. Daughtry Corbin that Dr. Abigail Callahan is calling."

Sailor grinned. "This is Sailor, Daughtry's sister. He's stepped out of the office for a bit, but I'd be happy to take a message and have him return your call."

"Stepped out, has he . . . more like ran away, I'd say!"

Sailor couldn't hold back a giggle. Oh boy, she thought, brother has met his match with Dr. Abigail Callahan. She imagined fireworks exploding when the doctor huffed out her disapproval over the situation and told Sailor if Dr. Corbin didn't return her call within the next half hour she'd send the *paddy wagon* to haul his sorry self back to South Dakota for their conversation.

Eyes glowing with the mental picture of her distinguished brother strapped in a paddy wagon, Sailor assured Abbie she'd relay the message asap. The phone went silent and Sailor bent double as the belly laughter spilled out of her in joyous wave after wave.

She'd finally been successful at composing herself when the office door opened about fifteen minutes later and Daughtry stopped at her desk to ask if there were any urgent phone messages he needed to return.

Sailor handed him the slip of paper with Abbie's name scrawled in big letters with a half dozen exclamation points lined up behind it. She never said a word as he took the slip of paper, sighed and closed his door with a resounding bang.

The laughter rolled in her belly for a second time as Sailor leaned back in her chair and laughed as quietly as possible until her eyes were running rivers of water.

. . .

Sailor finished her tasks at their office around three o'clock. Daughtry was still holed up in his office, door closed. Deciding to respect his privacy she beeped his phone. He didn't answer. She beeped it a second time, still no answer. Putting respect for his privacy aside she tapped on the closed door.

"Come on in, Sailor," he called in a muffled tone.

She opened the door to walk inside. Daughtry sat with his back to the door.

"Umm," Sailor cleared her throat and waited.

He slowly turned the chair around to face her. His usually calm expression looked like a dark thunderstorm just about to burst. Even though she'd not met the obvious cause of his attitude, a mental slideshow of a tiny red-haired beauty yielding a sword flashed in her imagination. It was so real, and so humorous that Sailor fought to restrain the laugher that threatened to gush out.

Instead of laughing, she went around to the back of the chair and wrapped her arms around his neck. "Aww, is someone having a rough day?"

Daughtry nodded.

Sailor pulled up a chair and sat. "You want to talk about it?"

He nodded again, his eyes lowered. "I feel as though my breath has been knocked out of me."

She smiled slightly at the admission which didn't need an explanation for her to understand.

"I feel your pain, Daughtry."

He took a breath, brows drawn into a look of pure misery. "Man, you too?"

Sailor smiled in sympathy and nodded yes.

19

Vickie called the next day before Sailor left to drive to the office. She was bubbling over with the wonder of her honeymoon in Charleston, South Carolina. Sailor listened without interrupting as Vickie gave brief snippets of their stay in rapid fire short sentences. She jumped from the description of the Bed and Breakfast where they'd stayed to the romantic walks along the Battery, and then to the southern cuisine served at ten different restaurants with such speed it had Sailor's head spinning like a merry-go-round at the fair.

When Vickie paused to take a breath, Sailor jumped into the conversation. "Wow, sounds like the perfect honeymoon."

Vickie sighed. "It was my dream come to life. Mason is the most amazing man. He planned every single day."

"Are you the same Vickie I know and love?"

She laughed. "Of course I am the same person. Well, except for being married, of course, well . . . you know, some things are different . . . that is . . . with being married . . ." Vickie's voice trailed off and Sailor saw the bright red blush that could so easily rise in Vickie's face when she was embarrassed.

"Well, that's not exactly where I was going with the conversation. I meant to say you are usually the person who plans every detail of a trip you take, so hearing you say that Mason planned it all just surprised me."

"Are you saying in a very nice way that I am a control freak?"

"No, I would call you more of a detail-oriented organized woman who knows her mind and goes after what she wants with all the gusto of an

Olympic hopeful with their eye on the gold medal." Sailor paused, "Speaking of control freaks, I think I may have met one today."

"Really, well do tell all."

Thirty minutes later Sailor hit the end button on her cell. She and Vickie had covered a lot of verbal ground during the chat. They had established that Charleston was the ideal location for honeymooners and Sailor had brought her up to date on Daughtry's friend Abbie, who in Sailor's opinion was a control freak. Vickie told her it wasn't fair to judge a person on one phone call and made her promise to keep an open mind about someone who might be a potential sister-in-law.

She eventually got around to telling Vickie about speaking to Daughtry and her parents about forgiveness and how extending forgiveness had began a healing in her own heart. The call wound down with Vickie promising to call her the next day as soon as Mason left for work.

By the time Sailor parked her car and opened the office door she rcalized she only had a week until she would be in Peron. The thought brought fear and excitement shivers all wrapped up in each other because she knew without a doubt the trip would determine her destiny.

A little ditty from a commercial she'd watched on television played in her mind as she prepared to open the office for business. *Should I stay or should I go?*

20

The week long stretch of grey skies and rain ended at last. The day opened with a glorious sunrise of surreal pinks and blues that chased away Sailor's doldrums. Mary called last night to tell her Frank didn't think she should drive to Peron alone and they would pick her up around ten o'clock the next morning. Even though Sailor was a grown woman and fully capable of driving to Georgia alone she agreed to ride with them out of respect for Frank's concern for her safety. The fact that she loved the older couple and enjoyed their company made it easy to say yes.

She'd met Frank and Mary Carter last year at Colton and Loren's house in Monroe. Since then, they'd taken her under their parental wings along with the other members of the Destiny Foundation. Mary's expertise as a veterinarian was well known for using the natural herbs as healing agents she'd learned from childhood as a member of the Cherokee Nation. Her family attended Community Church in Peron where Alex was pastor. Frank, a former detective in New York had fallen head over heels in love with Mary when a happenstance meeting brought them together in Monroe. Since then they had more or less mothered the group of younger people who'd become their family.

Sailor stared at the opened suitcases with more than two dozen outfits flung haphazard across them. Packing for a trip was never her favorite thing to do. She always ended up with more than she needed. Of course, she didn't know if the weather in North Georgia had lost its winter chill. Springtime in North Florida along the Gulf was a guessing game where the natives had learned to multi-layer clothing to accommodate whatever the weather sent their way on any particular day. Sailor smiled as she pictured the out-of-state beach goers who thought Florida was sunshine year round. Most of them ended up in the stores restocking their wardrobe when the chill drove them away from the beach.

"Ugh, I should have packed last night instead of watching *The Notebook* for the hundredth time." The movie was a favorite, and no matter how many times she watched it, she cried. It wasn't any different last night; the tears had fallen as the story of one man's love for a woman went beyond their differences and their obstacles in life. Sailor sobbed as he remained true to their love even when she could no longer recognize him due to the ravages of Alzheimer.

Love always finds a way . . . the thought popped in her mind as she looked at the beauty of the early morning sky outside her window. The sun was higher in the sky now, casting fingers of pearly-pink color farther across the whole sky.

Sailor recognized the still small voice inside her spirit. Communication was becoming easier, less stilted as she spoke the words written in her heart. "Lord I honor You this morning. I honor Your power and all that You create. I accept that You are working on my behalf and if Alex is to be a part of my destiny, I accept that as well. Open my eyes to see Your will."

Peacefulness eased across Sailor's face as she closed her conversation with God.

She decided multi-layering would work in Georgia weather just like in Florida. Choosing two outfits for each of the three days she'd be in Peron, she laid them in her suitcase and snapped it shut.

Sailor mentally checked off her list. Bills paid – leftovers thrown out – alarm set. She tapped her fingers on the bar, amused that she was worried about such things as leftovers in the refrigerator when she would only be gone less than a week. "Oh boy, here I am calling Abbie a control freak. Look at me . . .duh!"

Spooning the last bite of Special K yogurt and fruit cereal in her mouth, before she took the empty bowl along with her juice glass to the sink, Sailor swished them with Dawn and warm water. She dried them, put them away and gave the counter a final wipe.

The cell phone on the counter by the sink pinged letting her know she had a new text. Sailor dried her hands and opened the message. It was from Vickie. "Have a good time. Keep me in the loop."

She answered with a smiley face. A second later Daughtry's ringtone sounded.

"Good morning brother. You're up early."

He sounded gruff when he said, "Been up since daybreak. My sleeping patterns are confused. I keep waking up to South Dakota time."

"Well, remember its Wednesday and you don't open the office until one o'clock. Go back to sleep."

Daughtry lowered the tone of his voice. He spoke with the same calm and easy manner she was accustomed to hearing. She was still shocked at seeing his temper flare when Abbie Callahan had called last week. When he got truly angry, he was formidable. Sailor was a lot more comfortable with this side of his temperament.

"Here's the thing," he said in a soothing tone of voice. "I've thought about this all morning."

Sailor could only stare at the phone, mute.

Daughtry seemed to pick up on her reaction even though he couldn't see her face. He forged ahead despite Sailor's silence.

"As I said, I couldn't sleep so I've done some real soul searching and I wanted you to know the decision I've made before you leave on your trip today."

Sailor shivered. She knew her brother was a believer, but he didn't talk about his faith very often.

"Soul searching," she finally whispered.

"It's not a major announcement, Sailor. Not the start of a war or the end of the world or anything in that league."

Sailor's mind whirled back through the last few days and centered on the moment a scarlet-haired doctor had shaken her brother's world.

"This is about Abbie, am I correct?"

"Yes," he signed, still talking in a soft modulated voice. "You'll be home on Monday and can open the office. I booked a flight to South Dakota Sunday afternoon. Abbie is inside my head talking, challenging me at every turn. I need to see her face-to-face so I can figure out where this is going."

"I understand. That's why I'm going to Peron to see Alex. This is serious business and we need to see the person's faces when we are talking about matters that could affect the rest of our lives."

"You've got that right, Sailor. This is uncharted waters for both of us. So, here's wishing you the best. Promise you'll call if you run into a snag you can't handle."

Her tone softened as she recognized his need to let her know he was always there for her. "I promise and the same goes for me. You're my brother. Love you, Daughtry."

21

"Mary, come inside," Sailor exclaimed, grinning wide as she continued to think about her conversation with Daughtry.

Mary was gorgeous. Exotic looking with long dark hair and eyes such a deep brown the iris was swallowed in their depth. She felt the power of her gaze that somehow managed to radiate peace, with a feminine softness that belied her true strength.

She wrapped Sailor in an affectionate embrace. A subtle hint of lavender and a fragrance Sailor couldn't identify lingered in the air near Mary. Try as she could, Sailor could never put a name to the unique scent and had come to the conclusion it must be something secretive that Mary concocted from the herbs and flowers she used for healing.

Sailor melted into the motherly hug, appreciating how Frank and Mary had included her in their circle of love, no questions asked.

What would she do without them? Sailor knew they had her back. Her issues with trust had created a barrier around her heart that only allowed a few to break through its defenses. Mary had breached the barrier when they'd met at Loren's house in Monroe and every meeting since then had re-enforced the initial feeling of acceptance and trust.

Mary held her at arm's length. "Are you as excited as me?" Her eyes danced as she told Frank to grab the suitcase Sailor had placed by the door.

Sailor pulled the door shut and listened for the lock to click. She followed Frank and Mary to their Jeep Cherokee and slid into the back seat. Mary turned to look at Sailor.

"I left Loren and Carolyn on turtle watch. You know the Loggerhead sea turtles are coming ashore now to lay their eggs. Frank and I are members of the volunteer group who patrol the shoreline from Monroe all the way to St. George Island."

"I can't believe I've never seen the little hatchlings emerge from their nest in the beach sand," Sailor lamented.

Frank slid under the steering wheel and turned the key. The jeep motor sounded, its engine purring softly.

"What did I miss?" he asked

She and Mary laughed at the Papa Bear tone of his voice.

Mary laid her hand on his shoulder. "You sweet man, you're always ready to take on the world for those you care about."

He slid the gear into drive and the jeep responded smoothly as he joined the early morning traffic out of Tallahassee to Interstate 75.

Sailor sat forward in the seat. "I was lamenting the fact that I've lived in Tallahassee for several years and never took the time to see the Loggerhead sea turtles during the nesting season."

"It's a sight to behold," Frank said. "I've driven to St. George Island a few times to see them leaving the nest. It's unbelievable to watch hundreds of tiny turtles about two inches long scurrying toward the surf to begin their voyage in life. Of course, now that Mary and I are turtle watch volunteers we see their beginning in the deep holes their mamas dig to lay eggs in the wet sand. Just yesterday I followed the trail the loggerhead left in the sand and found a nest to mark with the *Do Not Destroy Sea Turtle Nest* sign."

Mary's face softened. "It is like a spiritual oneness with God as you watch the tiny turtles tumble out of the nest to race across the wet sand led by an instinct passed down for millions of years. If all goes well and they are not misled by human distractions they fix their eyes on the light of the horizon where the sky meets the sea and dive into the Gulf water to be pulled out by the rolling waves." She turned towards Sailor. "You must come for a visit when we return from Georgia. It will touch your soul and leave a mark of remembrance that can never be erased."

. . .

Sailor tried to follow Frank and Mary's conversation but her mind continued to drift back to Mary's comment about the turtle migration leaving a mark on your soul. Lord knows her soul had taken a beating in the past with things that had left ugly marks. In the last weeks she had come to the understanding that God had not forsaken her, even during the most horrible day of her life when the cruelty of rape had carved scars into her soul so deep she'd never dreamed they could heal. She shuddered. She couldn't imagine a worst fate for anyone.

Sailor saw rather than heard her phone light up with an incoming call. It was Alex. She pressed accept, feeling a churning in her stomach. "Alex, how nice of you to call."

There was a slight pause. "Sailor, I don't mean to speak preacher talk and scare you, but as I was praying just now your beautiful face came to mind and I heard God speak to my spirit, "Call Sailor and tell her that I will guide her steps into the rushing waves of life just as I guide the fledging turtles toward their life's destiny. All that's required is to believe."

Something stirred in Mary causing her to glance at Sailor even though she didn't want to intrude on her phone call.

Mary smiled. Sailor had such an expressive face. She knew the moment the answer came to her. There was relief and lessening of grief followed by a look of wonder.

She caught Sailor's eye. "Good news?"

Sailor's lips trembled. "Yes, very good news."

22

Later that afternoon, Frank exited the interstate and made the turn towards Peron. Sailor felt jittery as she watched the familiar landmarks of the historic town. The sky was a piercing blue. For as far as she could see, green lawns and beautifully kept flower gardens swirled together with as much color and energy as a painting by van Gogh. The view was different from the bustle of Tallahassee, yet she felt a kinship with the town she'd only visited once during Colton and Loren's wedding. The mystery and magic of the Georgia town conjured up scenes from history books she'd read describing the horrific battles of the Civil War fought there and the steadfastness of the people like Mary and Loren's ancestors who had forged a thriving community out of the ashes of the aftermath of war.

"Do you want to go by Alex's house or to the hotel," Mary asked.

"Take me to the hotel. I'll call Alex and let him know we've arrived."

Sailor pulled out her wallet. "Let me pay my part on the expenses of the trip here."

Mary wagged her hand at Sailor. "Absolutely not. We were making the trip anyway, and we've enjoyed your company during the drive."

Frank stopped the Jeep at the red light. Traffic was light as cars moved slowly down the other lane of the main street. Sailor watched a group of afternoon shoppers who appeared to be in friendly conversations.

Sailor said, "Please tell David, Jessie and Mary Rose hello, and that I want to spend some time with them if possible."

"I've already took the liberty of planning a picnic on our family mountain and of course you and Alex are invited to join us."

"Thank you, I'm sure Alex will welcome the opportunity to visit your family homestead. I know I will. It's breathtaking in the meadow. I wouldn't want to leave Peron without honoring your grandmother Mary by laying flowers at her grave."

Mary nodded. "Tell Alex we'll see him at the parade Saturday morning. We'll meet in Mary's Meadow at one o'clock for lunch, so plan to spend the whole afternoon with the Cook family." Mary laughed with humor. "You know how the braves in our family like to compete. There aren't battles to be fought in these modern times so they play their battle games by trying to tell the most outrageous tales of bravery."

Sailor burst out laughing. "Oh, I do remember those stories from the last time we were here. I loved every one of them and can't wait to see what they come up with this time."

Frank turned into the driveway of the Marriott Hotel. He put the car in park and jumped out to get Sailor's luggage from the back of the Jeep. He turned to set it on the sidewalk just as a porter pushed a luggage cart up beside him.

"Thanks, young man."

The porter doffed his hat in reply and waited for Sailor to step out of the Jeep.

"Thank you both so much for the pleasant trip. I'll call you and let you know where we are at the parade."

"Sounds perfect." Mary laughed. "You'll probably spot us right away. David asked that we all wear our native clothing for the day since we are going to have tribal council up at Mary's mountain home after the festivities in town."

"Oh, I can't wait to see the Cook families again dressed to the nines like you were for your wedding day," Sailor said.

The porter waited for her to say goodbye to Frank and Mary and then Sailor followed him inside to the registration desk. The lobby was crowded with folks trying to secure a room at the last minute for the weekend Blossom Festival. She was thankful Alex had called and made reservations for her.

Sailor smiled as she passed a family of eight children sitting on their luggage like a set of doorsteps. She heard their Mom and Dad negotiating with the desk clerk for a room and she breathed a silent prayer to God on their behalf that they would have a room for them.

When the elevator door opened, Sailor waited for a half-dozen people to unload and then followed the porter inside the elevator to go to her room on the second floor. She caught a glimpse of the children as the elevator door closed and waved. They waved back at her and all of a sudden she pictured a set of twin girls with shiny light brown hair and sky blue eyes who looked identical to Alex. Sailor's breath caught in her throat as she imagined the beautiful children were her own. It was a new experience for Sailor who had never let her thoughts dwell on the possibility of being a mother. Her feelings of being damaged goods had blocked any hope of becoming a wife and a mother – but yet, here she was toying with the idea it could become reality.

The elevator dinged and the door slid open interrupting her daydreaming. The porter stopped outside her room and placed her suitcase on the floor. She tipped him before slipping the pass card into the lock to open the door.

Pushing the door closed with her foot, Sailor admired the room decorated in neutral tones with a touch of deep forest green for accent. A bouquet of red roses sat on a round table in the center of the room. Not accustomed to such a personal touch at a hotel, Sailor walked over to breathe in the fragrance of the luscious blooms. Nestled in the roses was a small white card with her name written there. Underneath her name it was signed, Love Alex. She reached for the card and heard her cell signaling an incoming call from inside her handbag.

It was Alex. "You sent me roses."

Alex chuckled, obviously delighted that she was pleased with his gift.

"How do you know it was me? Maybe you have another secret admirer named Alex."

Sailor's heart melted with his kindness. "You sent me roses," she repeated and then started to weep.

Alex heard the crack in her voice and the soft sound of her tears falling. It tore him up inside. He was appalled to think he'd done something to hurt her when he had meant to bless her by showing his love with a gift of red roses.

"Oh, Lord, I didn't mean to cause you to cry. Sailor . . . sweet Sailor, I sent the roses to make you feel welcome in my town and because they remind me of your beauty. You are like a perfect rose to me, so full of life and fragrance that perfumes the air wherever you are."

Sailor hiccupped. She wiped the tears with the back of her hand and said, "You wonderful man. These are not unhappy tears, these are happy tears. I'm overwhelmed with your gift of thoughtfulness. No one has ever sent me roses."

Alex stood up taller, squared his shoulders and felt like he could take on the entire world. "Well, darling, I promise you this bouquet is just one of many. I'll buy you roses every day of the year for the rest of our lives if it makes you happy."

. . .

She heard the light tap on the door and knew it was Alex. He'd phoned to tell her he was in the hotel lobby and on the way up to her room. She glanced in the mirror as she passed it on the way to the door. She felt like a preteen, worried that her dress and hair was not appropriate to have dinner with a pastor. Chiding herself for having such silly thoughts, Sailor opened the door and he was there. So close . . . She looked at him intently and thought about the way he made her feel – alive again, cherished. But she didn't want to analyze her feelings anymore, or worry about complications or what would or would not happen in the future.

She wanted to think of some clever comment. "Hey, Preacher Man, how about we paint the town red tonight." Or maybe, "You must be slumming with damaged goods tonight. Better not get caught by any church board members!"

Oh, that was bad! Thank God she hadn't said it out loud.

He was still there, and he smiled slowly, as if he was waiting. She inhaled a breath and stepped forward so they were almost touching.

But, when she moved, he moved too, and once again his eyes, those beautiful blue eyes, with tiny flecks of brown, were on hers. She moved into his arms. And he kissed her. It was a burst of something so exquisite, so sweet, something she never expected to feel. She prayed the past was gone and this unexplainable glorious feeling could be her future.

It was a beautiful kiss. Full of desire, hunger, and promises.

Then he broke away and they both took in several ragged breaths.

They still didn't speak, just joined hands and quietly walked to the elevator, still caught up in the wonder of what had just happened.

23

The morning after her date with Alex, Sailor was still walking in the afterglow of their time together. Alex was picking her up around 10 o'clock for the parade and picnic. She hummed to herself as she dressed in white capris, a lemon-yellow polo shirt and Converse shoes, and then brushed her silky black hair and pulled it into a loose topknot on her head.

She'd called room service as soon as the kitchen opened and had them bring her a pot of hot tea, a bagel and red grapes. Too nervous to eat, she sat and munched her light breakfast and remembered her night with Alex as she waited.

He had taken her to an upscale restaurant that served one of the best rib-eye steaks she had ever eaten. The term *so tender you could cut it with a fork* was aptly applied when Sailor tested its authenticity and found it to be true. The ambience of the restaurant was wonderful, but it was Alex's company that had filled her entire being with happiness she'd rarely experienced in her lifetime.

They had not discussed *the kiss*, but Sailor could still feel the soft touch of his lips upon her own. She'd been kissed numerous times, but those kisses had always left her feeling soiled and totally lacking in enjoyment. Truth be known, she'd always come home and get in a hot shower to scrub away the touch of another person on her body. But, it was different with Alex. She longed to feel his warm lips and gentle touch against her skin again.

She was thrilled when Alex asked her to take the moonlight carriage ride that was part of the week-end festivities in Peron. The kindly driver was attired in a suit reminiscent of days from long ago and offered his arm in support as Sailor climbed into the white carriage. Alex slipped in beside her and the handsome black horse took off in a gentle trot.

The starlit sky covered them like a soft blanket. Large Oak trees with sprawling branches made shadowy silhouettes against the night sky, framed by the moonlight's glow. It was so peaceful; Sailor had relaxed with contentment and laid her head on Alex's shoulder.

He took her hand and traced the shape of a heart in her palm with his strong but gentle fingertip. "Sailor, the Bible tells us that God loves us so much He has engraved our names in the palm of His hand. As His creation we are blessed to feel a fraction of the emotion He created." He placed her hand against his chest and she felt the gentle beat of his heart. "True love comes from God and although I don't have the ability to eternally carve your name on my hand, I must tell you that you are eternally engraved on my heart. I love you tonight and I will love you forever."

The remnants of self-doubt had fallen in jagged slivers from her heart. His declaration of love had taken the raw places left behind and bound them up with the warm salve of the kind words poured from his heart. For the first time in her life she felt trust in a man and knew he would never judge her as less than perfect because of one horrible event that had marked her as imperfect.

Her heart had thumped in her chest when he'd wrapped his arms around her and pressed a kiss to her lips. His love made her realize she was no longer the child that had lay on the wet ground and listened to the taunting catcalls and slurs those boys had hurled at her on that fateful afternoon when she was twelve years old. They had stripped away every ounce of self-respect from her soul. But, somehow, Alex had brought healing instead of injury, wholeness instead of cutting her self-esteem to shreds."

"Alex," she'd pleaded. "Please, if I tell you something do you promise not to judge me?"

He'd brushed the hair from her brow with tenderness as she brokenly told him about the day her life had forever been altered. She didn't hold anything back.

By the time the carriage had made its journey through town, she had poured out the vile memories locked deep in her heart. Alex had listened without interrupting, but he never moved away from her. He had held her tenderly, offering comfort as she poured out all the sordid details.

When she'd run out of words, he'd asked her if she'd forgiven herself. His question had startled her and she'd felt a moment of panic. Then he'd explained how humans tend to take responsibility for bad things that happen to them even though they have absolutely no control over the situation. He'd said many times we can accept God's forgiveness, and even others forgiveness, but we have a hard time forgiving ourselves.

She'd wept at his gentle and wise words that had given her the courage to believe, to be able to see the light of hope shining in her future . . . a future that included Pastor Alex Collins.

. . .

Alex had never been so totally beguiled by a woman. He'd known Sailor for almost a year and most of their time together was spent in group gatherings, but he was still enchanted. She was like the sunrise, reliable, yet ever-changing, always magnificent.

He whistled softly as he stepped into the elevator with several people. The buzz of conversation swirled around him as the door closed. Seconds later, an elderly couple stepped out of the elevator ahead of him. He noticed the caring way the gentleman held the lady's arm. It was such a protective gesture. *I can see Sailor and me together at that age . . .* the thought drifted through his mind and made him hasten his steps down the hall to her room.

The door opened on his first knock. The static electricity sizzled in the air. Neither spoke for a moment, but let their eyes do the talking. Then Alex grinned, happiness spreading across his handsome face. His blue eyes were lit from within as he took in every detail of the woman facing him. Finally, he cleared his throat and struggled to find his voice that had gone in hiding in the face of such intense emotion.

"Are you ready for a day of fun and games?"

Hearing his voice, Sailor's knees suddenly went weak. She leaned against the door facing to keep from falling at his feet. Blast it all, how could the mere sound of his voice have this effect on her? Could she possibly be in love with him? How in the world was she supposed to know what being in love felt like?

She straightened up and mumbled, "Fun and games?"

The silly grin widened. "You know. I'm here to take you to the parade." He touched her forehead and asked with sudden concern, "Are you okay?"

She giggled and felt the giggle trace all the way from the top of her head to the bottom of her feet. She wanted to shout, "I'm okay as long as I'm with you!"

. . .

Sailor felt like she was walking about a foot off the ground as Alex proudly escorted her down the crowded sidewalk in downtown Peron.

He stopped ever so often to introduce her to folks, many of whom were members of his church. Coming face to face with them made her a little nervous. She was still concerned about attending church services at Community Church on Sunday. Things were more than all right with her and Alex after she'd confessed her deepest secrets to him last night. He had encouraged her to lay it all at Jesus' feet and promise never to pick up the burden of guilt she'd carried inside for so many years. She wondered why meeting people from his church had suddenly caused her insecurities to resurface.

Sailor frowned and Alex, attuned to her body language felt her arm tremble.

"What's wrong," he whispered in her ear. She smiled at him and fought to hold back the tears that wanted to spring from her eyes. *Lord help me, I don't want to embarrass Alex in front of his church members.* Thank God, her silent plea calmed her enough to stop the threatening tears.

Alex nodded and wrapped his arm around her shoulders. He spotted the Cook family arrayed in

160

their Native American garb clustered together near the City Hall building.

"Look, Sailor, there's Mary and Frank with the whole tribe."

"I see them. They look stunning. Can we go over to say hi?"

As they approached the Cook family, the sirens on the police car and fire truck pierced the cool clear air of the pleasant Georgia morning signaling the start of the parade. Children moved closer to the edge of the sidewalks in anticipation Sailor was lifted out of her dark moment of doubt by the shouts of excited chatter from the children lining the street.

Dark thoughts had no place on this beautiful morning when she was surrounded with good friends and happy children.

The past was the past and she refused to let it intrude on one of the happiest days of her life.

24

Sailor checked the time on the phone again. Ten o'clock, only a half-hour had passed since she'd checked it last. She had awakened with the sunrise, thrown the covers aside and padded across the carpet with bare feet to stand at the window and watch the darkness slip away. It was replaced with streaks of pinks, yellows and lavender of a beautiful morning. The wonder of awakening with such hope in her heart was re-enforced by God's palette of color flung across the Georgia sky, painting a masterpiece that only he could paint anew each morning.

It would be a day of many first -- the first time to attend Community Church -- the first time to hear Alex give a sermon from the pulpit, and the first time to meet his congregation as someone who was an integral part of his life.

Obviously nervous, Sailor checked her appearance in the mirror. She saw someone dressed tastefully in a white lace covered dress, fitted snugly around her waist and falling in graceful folds to just below her knees. She had brushed her naturally curly hair away from her face and secured each side with turquoise combs that were a gift from Mary. White ballerina flats completed her outfit. She decided against any jewelry, choosing to let the beautiful handmade combs made by one of Mary's Cherokee relatives take center stage. Their simplistic beauty was enough.

She checked the time again . . . almost time for Alex to pick her up for the church service.

Turning the cell phone face down on the table, Sailor went to get the bottle of water she'd had room service bring up with her breakfast. The cool water slid down her throat erasing the dry scratchy feeling.

She heard a knock at the door and spun around to open it.

Alex was there.

She recognized the suit and shirt he was wearing. It was the same one he'd wore when he performed the marriage ceremony for Mason and Vickie.

He grimaced, as if reading her mind. "It's my favorite suit."

"It's a great suit," she told him. "And you wear it well."

"I thank you. And I might add, you're lovely in that white dress, in fact, I'm not sure I need to take you out in public for fear that someone will kidnap you away from me."

Sailor laughed.

"Sorry, I'm not very good at flirting. That was corny."

She laughed again, and held her head at an angle, studying him. "I like corny. It was just what I need to get rid of the jitters marching inside my stomach."

Alex smiled. "You're going to love the good people at Community Church, Sailor, and they're going to love you. Just be the beautiful woman God created you to be and everything will turn out just right."

He offered his hand and she placed her hand in his. Alex closed his long fingers securely around her smaller hand. It was like coming home. He was her safe harbor, and she instinctively knew he would always be there to catch her when the tempestuous swells of life attempted to drown her with insecurity and doubts.

She marveled at the kindness and patience of this man that had wooed her so gently. He'd confessed the night they talked that he was smitten from the first time he saw her at Loren's house in Monroe. He said she reminded him of a little bird he'd discovered in the woods near his home when he was a small boy. When he'd first noticed the bird it looked as if it was okay, but when he walked closer he saw that one of its wings was at an odd angle as it helplessly fluttered on the ground. No matter how many times the little bird attempted to gain altitude the broken wing kept it earthbound.

He told her he'd sat beside the little bird for over an hour, talking to it until finally the bird trusted him enough he was able to pick it up. He'd said he still remembered the feel of the tiny bird quivering in his hand and how he'd vowed to protect it and love it until it was whole again and could soar into the sky like God had created it to soar.

Then he'd held Sailor close and told her he recognized the same wary look of fear in her spirit as he'd seen in the bird, but if she'd trust him he'd protect her and do everything in his power to help her be all that God had created her to be. He'd lifted her face in his hand and said, "One day, when you're ready, it will make me the happiest man on earth if you agree to be my wife."

She'd whispered, "Soon, Alex, very soon."

They rode the elevator down and walked out into the brisk spring morning, Alex stayed close, never letting go of her hand until he'd opened the door of his late model sedan and she'd slipped inside on the soft leather seat.

The faint scent of Alex's cologne lingered in the car. Sailor closed her eyes enjoying the pleasant fragrance of the woodsy aroma. It intensified when Alex opened the driver's side door and got inside.

"This is a day of first for me."

"Why is that?"

"Well, for one thing I've never been driven to church in a preacher's car," Sailor told him.

He answered her with a wide grin and she felt its soothing effect all the way down to her toes that curled in response inside her shoes.

On the short drive Alex told her about his church members, some of whom she'd met at the parade the day before. He said for the most part they were hard-working salt of the earth people who loved God and their fellow man. He shared a couple of humorous stories about his first days in the pulpit when he'd stepped on a few of the deacon's toes and they'd felt the need to tone his fiery sermons down to suit their agendas.

"Every church deals with personality conflicts, but God is faithful."

"Will those deacons be there today," Sailor asked with concern.

He heard the rise of fear in her question. "Sure they will, they've appointed themselves the moral conscience of the congregation." He saw her look of panic. "Don't worry, my lady, I will slay the dragons for you."

As Alex drove the car into the open carport of the parsonage next door to the church, Sailor saw several cars in the parking area in front of the church. Her heart thundered in her chest as she imagined every eye staring at her when she walked inside.

Her voice quivered when she told Alex, "I don't think I can do this."

He turned to her and wrapped his arm around her very gently. "Sailor, I'll never force you to go beyond what you choose to do, but, remember the God we serve will never bring us to a place in our lives and then abandon us to deal with it on our own."

Sailor said, "Why do I do this Alex? I move forward one step and then take two steps backwards. It makes me so angry with myself."

He stroked her cheek with the back of his hand. She felt the peace and calmness that she'd come to realize was one of his gifts from God.

"I'm sorry. I'm keeping you from your duties as a pastor."

"Never. Being a pastor is more than standing behind a pulpit and delivering a good sermon. Jesus taught by example that the world is our congregation and we are to bind up the hurting wherever the opportunity presents itself."

Love for Alex burst inside Sailor and she literally melted against his strong body. "You are a good man, Alex. You make me believe I can be everything you deserve. It's just taking a little while for me to get there."

"I have all the time in the world for you, Sailor. You are my destiny."

She moved to open the car door, but Alex stopped her. "Wait just a moment. I want to tell you about Melodie."

Sailor turned to face him.

Alex paused and then sighed deeply. "Melodie is a beautiful young girl that had a similar experience as you this past year. Like you, she was twelve when she was raped. But hers didn't come at the hands of reckless boys, hers came from a trusted family member. She had to endure being removed from the only home and family she'd ever known and placed in foster care. As if that wasn't enough pain, she had to suffer the humiliation of court hearings that exposed her shame to the whole world. She won't allow anyone to touch her and hasn't spoken a word since she made the 911 call to tell the police what had happened."

Sailor winced under the pain. "Oh my God!"

She sat in stunned silence until Alex opened the door. She took his hand. His touch was strong, yet oh so gentle. As he'd told her about Melodie she understood the awesome calling and the compassion for others that God had placed in his life, and she was humbled that he wanted her to be a part of something so amazing.

Sailor saw a group of four people approaching the front door of the church just ahead of them. They turned and called, "Good morning, Pastor Alex."

Alex waved at them, and then gave Sailor an encouraging look. "Let's do this!" he said.

They walked inside and were soon surrounded with folks shaking hands, hugging necks, and sharing good morning and how are you greetings. The overall feeling to Sailor was one of good cheer from a group of people who seemed to genuinely care about each other.

The feeling of acceptance stayed with her until she and Alex walked to the front of the church and she looked out at the congregation. The pulse in her neck throbbed with renewed panic. Dear God, her face was the only face of color in the entire building. She was looking at a sea of faces as white as the foam that rode the waves of the Gulf to the shore.

Alex felt her clench her fingers inside his hand. The chatter stopped. It was absolute silence inside the church.

He didn't let go of her hand, but lifted his other arm towards heaven and prayed. "Dear God, we thank you for the opportunity to gather in Your house on the beautiful Lord's Day and we pray that each of us will invite Your Presence to join us as we offer our praise and thankfulness to You. In Jesus name, Amen."

Silence remained. Not one person stirred, and Sailor felt every eye boring into her. It was painful. She wanted to run from their accusing eyes!

Alex squeezed her hand, trying to reassure her.

The seconds ticked in the silence and her heartbeat raced, almost cutting off the flow of life-giving breath in her body.

And, Alex held her hand firmly in his.

His beautiful deep voice rang out, dispelling the silence. "Community Church, we have a special guest with us this morning. Some of you met her yesterday at the celebration downtown, but for those who've not had the pleasure, I'd like to introduce, Miss Sailor Corbin from Tallahassee."

He drew her closer to his side. "I'd also like to add, that she is an answer to my prayer and I sincerely hope she will agree to be my wife in the very near future."

Sailor felt faint, her breath trapped inside her chest.

Still silence . . . no one moved until a beautiful girl, with hair the color of spun gold stood at the back of the church. She slowly walked down the center aisle. As she neared the front the entire congregation stood.

She stopped before the altar and Sailor looked into her green eyes that were glistening with tears. Her eyes reminded Sailor of priceless polished Jade, worth millions of dollars. They bore deep into Sailors' soul with empathy like Sailor had never experienced. It released the tension in her and she felt it fly away and disappear into a puff of nothingness.

Everyone held their breath . . . waiting to see what would happen next.

Alex spoke softly. "Sailor, this is Melodie."

Hot tears flowed down Sailor's cheeks. She was unsure of what to do. This was Melodie, the child Alex had mentioned. The one who was raped . . . The one, who would not allow anyone's touch, who had not spoken in over a year.

Melodie, bowed her head and dipped low to offer Sailor a curtsy as if she were standing before royalty.

A soft sound of awe swept the people and they instinctively leaned forward to watch what many would later call a miracle.

The severely wounded Melodie stepped onto the platform and wrapped her arms around Sailor's waist. The impact of her acceptance covered Sailor like warm oil. Its healing power flowed from the throne of God, through this child, filling Sailor with unspeakable love.

She was made whole at that moment.

But, the miracle didn't end there. God had a bigger plan. Melodie's voice rang out to touch everyone in the church as she sang the words to the beloved hymn, *Amazing Grace, how sweet the sound, that saved a wretch like me . . . I once was lost but now I'm found, twas blind, but now I see . . .*

All the hurt, un-forgiveness, disappointments, mistakes, and cultural differences faded as Sailor allowed her heart to embrace the future. She was no longer a woman of color in a sea of white, nor was she a tiny bird with a broken wing who couldn't fly. She was a daughter of God who had come to a small church made up of good people who recognized God had chosen to visit on an ordinary Sunday morning.

And, she gained an added blessing when her inner spirit clearly heard the voice of God whisper . . . this is your daughter, she rescued you, now you can rescue her.

Alex embraced them as the congregation joined with them to sing the remaining verses of Amazing Grace.

Sailor's destiny had brought her home.

Acknowledgements

This story is what it is because of several special people, and I would like to thank them for everything they've done.

To Leta Turner and Jonnie Whittington, my wonderful editors, Thank you for the many hours you spent editing. I will be forever grateful for everything you've done.

To Monica L. Walker, thank you for sharing your artistic genius with a camera. You captured the perfect sunrise for Sailor's story.

To Jason Taylor, whose computer skills excel. Thank you for your humor, and your good-hearted nature. I truly appreciate you.

To Writers INK, my writing buddies who make this journey enjoyable every week.

I want to thank The Thomas County Historical Society for information used in this book about the Rose Festival.

Other Life-Changing Fiction by

Delores Leggett Walker

Promise Series

Legend of Promise

Gathering Promises

Promises Kept

www.facebook.com/promiseseries

Made in the USA
Charleston, SC
22 August 2016